INVASION OF THE EARTHMEN

∇

Vitor Rodrigues

To My Beloved Wife

Who felt, believed
And supported me,

And To All

Who believe
In the expansion
Of human consciousness.

ISBN: 978-0-9568833-8-4

~ 2nd Edition ~
Cover image credit: NASA/JPL
Original translation by Linda Pereira
Published in 2014 by Inner Vision Press

**Additional copies of this book can be purchased or ordered online at
Barnes and Noble, Amazon, WHSmith, Waterstones
and over the counter at most good book stores.**

www.InnerVisionPress.com

Contents

Chapter 1

Preparation

Gael leant back against a large tree and crossed her legs. She looked, listened, smelt, felt around her. As always, contact with the earth and cool grass felt good, the delicate aromas of the plants, the solid, calm strength of the trunk against which she leant and, within, the sap and metabolic vibration... She admired the familiar landscape. There were always subtle nuances in the hues of the plants and rocks, in the undulation of the wind, the shadows cast by the sun and the way in which its nourishing light struck the planet. Smiling, she breathed in the fresh air, feeling it gently make its way through to her lungs as she concentrated on the different groups of muscles in her body, one by one relaxing them, all trace of stiffness ebbing away. This was not hard to do since even in her natural state she was flexible, flowing, able to "dance with any ambience", as Axor, her master, liked to observe.

She breathed in deeply, slowly, as she withdrew into herself. Her energy, channelled towards her centre, feeding only her body's physical support systems. A fleeting, gentle shift in her interior world, and then the renewed sensation that nothing had really changed. The echoes and images of the natural world around her quickly began to fade, as if they belonged to another time or another place. Her body, her facial expression, took on the fixed features of the figures produced from the imaginations of sculptors. As her inner retreat continued, she scanned her emotional system for points of worry or fixation, for disturbances flowing outwards from the centre of the Being. Then she did the same with her mental system. All focal points of distraction, any worries that might draw her to the outside, were carefully but quickly tuned out. The natural energy of the setting flowed through her body, mingling with the vibrations she felt descend from her favourite star and the Ixnorian sun, and Gael attuned herself further to the planet's geomagnetic centre, her body quivering in response to the profound qualities of the cosmic energy emanating from within. Inside, the physical earth responded to the spiritual sky whilst the loving, welcoming nature of the exterior deepened the wisdom of the exchange. Finally, in the silence, Gael's vigilant will brought her down to her deepest self. In a state of heightened awareness, she contemplated recent events.

A huge ship had entered orbit. Since the visitors had acquired the knowledge necessary for translocation and interstellar travel, they appeared well suited for a mutually enriching contact. This was not surprising, though, as translocation required special psychic abilities on the part of travellers - active innocuity, unlimited perspective and simple love (regardless of the mental and emotional complexities that bound such love to hopes, desires or dreams limited by time and space) without such a condition, it would not be possible to "tune in" to far away points in the universe and instantaneously traverse the immeasurable distances involved. The Planetary Council of Ixnor had decided to welcome the newcomers with the serene respect worthy of any visitor on the assumption that they were civilised. The ship had been allowed to approach freely, the Ixnorians looking forward to the prospect of making contact with a new form of life, hitherto unknown children of the Cosmos. And Ixnorian ethics dictated that any display of mistrust would suggest a certain hostility and was therefore to be avoided. Trust was seen as the best "way to the heart" of newcomers, as adopting any other attitude before contact had been made would give rise to negative expectations and thus to an unjust assessment. Consequently the whole population had displayed the inner gesture of a benevolent host. Gael, the Interplanetary Welcoming Co-ordinator, had been appointed to represent the Council at the first contact and find out the intentions of the visitors. She had therefore communicated with the ship and briefed those responsible on a suitable landing place for their vehicle providing information on the firmness of the terrain, atmospheric and meteorological data. She was familiar with the language of the earthmen, as the sono-visual device they had provided had given her a chance to study it. The device was accompanied with recordings explaining the language through association, with detailed information included on the interrelation between forms and words, and examples of basic interaction between speakers. Although these seemed extremely simple and unable to reflect what was probably the true spiritual richness of the visitors, they were sufficient for an initial vocal encounter. It was typical of the Ixnorians to want to avoid imposing any norms as far as communication was concerned and, if the earthmen had indicated a preference for vocal exchange, then this would be respected - even if it seemed a rather poor form of communication. Indeed, it was always possible that the visitors possessed special, as yet unknown techniques of vocalisation. Gael was reminded of the singing gardeners of Zixus, whose cheerful, harmonious canticles helped accelerate the growth of stunningly beautiful flowers.

The centre of the Norya plateau had been chosen for the landing. Gael knew the area well: several times she had had the pleasure and the honour of welcoming beings from her own and other galaxies at this same spot. She loved it as much for its beauty as its geobiological value. The plateau was the highest region on the planet, rich in rock crystals and deep salt deposits - both excellent accumulators of biopsychic energy.

And, indeed, the energy in this zone of the planet was welcoming, nutritional, life-supporting - something that was usually appreciated by visitors from other worlds who, on landing here, felt cocooned in a pleasant, relaxing and invigorating atmosphere. The lush vegetation that covered the plateau hinted at its biomagnetic qualities: there were numerous tall trees and strikingly coloured plants, born from this energy and the mineral wealth of the area - two sides of the same coin, after all. Around the central clearing, on the edge of which stood the Co-ordinator, the trees spread out in radial fashion creating a natural marker that was easily visible from the air. The Ixnorians had had no need to influence the ways of this natural world since it fully served their purposes. The site chosen for the landing, ringed by carefully polished rocks, was exactly one kilometre in diameter and emitted a brilliant glow, a multi-coloured reflection of the natural force concentrated there. And all around, amongst the trees, grew pink and purple-blue flowers.

The landing area had been marked out with a luminous reproduction of the symbol chosen by the earthmen to identify themselves as space travellers. This contained a schematic reproduction of their solar system and showed the position of the planet Earth within it. Although very little was known about Earth culture, they believed that this gesture - as had happened on other occasions - could be taken as the equivalent of a friendly greeting: "Look, we have adopted one of your emblems. This planet is a home for you. We bid you welcome and are ready to learn with you".

In the silence, Gael sought the correct inner posture. She needed to ignore any initial opinions she might have formed regarding the visitors as these might prejudice her receptivity. The inner flow of love should become wholly simple and attentive. So the Interplanetary Welcoming Co-ordinator blocked out her thoughts concerning the reasons why the ship was so large or the impression of opaqueness she had felt watching it on the monitors. Likewise, she ignored the unpleasant feeling the tone of voice of the speaker had instilled in her at the first official contact. She entered a state of positive expectancy and felt a pleasant tension run through her. With it, she found total readiness. She was now free of any form of bias, open to new concepts and able to work together. Her spirit opened like a flower of constructive love. As for communication, it could be worked into filigrees of resplendent sharing.

Chapter 2

Approach

On board the Earth spaceship, Hamilton Burns was worried.

"Damn, Jim, something feels wrong. The only identification they asked for was our names. No questions about the ship, our weapons, our planet or the reasons for this expedition. Hell, they asked practically nothing! All they did was suggest a meeting between the representatives and a landing site for the exploration vessel. That's it. I don't know about you, but to me that definitely smells fishy."

Commander Burns was a cautious man, but also very confident in his skills. He would never walk away from a fight or from his duty whether to family, friends or country. With an athletic build, thick blonde hair and an aquiline nose, his features and gestures were equally exuberant. His easy chatter and penetrating, expressive blue eyes had captured and captivated the attention of many women on Earth.

He was considered quite a catch. He was also an experienced military commander and had been a member of various intervention groups, leading several American squadrons during the 2001 Arab-

American war. The medals he had been awarded were proof of his abilities. He had played an important part in the destruction of the sonic weapon arsenal which had almost handed victory to the Arabs. His in-depth knowledge of astronautics and translocation physics made him an even more suitable candidate for mission leader. And the fact that he was single meant leaving no close family behind.

"I agree, Commander. But we have no idea how they think. And we've been unable to detect any signs of military preparations. There have been no movements on the planet surface since we arrived. They appear to have no weapons at all. Perhaps they aren't that advanced. Look at the surface, see how dense and widespread the vegetation is. There are hardly any buildings, and the ones we can make out on our monitors are built of natural materials. The atmosphere is extraordinarily pure. I suppose ours must have been like this when our ancestors wore loincloths, carried clubs and ate raw meat. I'd suggest this is not such a technologically advanced people."

"No weapons and not advanced? Christ, you're naive. How do you explain the speed at which they learnt our language and answered us? Maybe they flush out the pollution and draw in pure air from another planet. And what about that weird crystal structure? Who knows what that's used for? But don't tell me it was built without the help of advanced technology. Besides, have you seen the number of ships they've got? They're small but autonomous, and don't appear to give off any detectable vibrations or heat. How on earth do they fly?"

Jim Dawson, Hamilton's second-in-command, fell silent for a few minutes. He also felt uncomfortable with the situation, but for slightly different reasons. Although he had plenty of combat experience, his training was fundamentally in military psychology and anthropology. He was finding it hard to understand the mentality of the aliens they were about to meet. They obviously preferred a face-to-face encounter rather than waste time simply dialoguing. That seemed tremendously careless of them, however. Hell, if this happened on Earth and a great star ship approached, prior contact and communication would be lengthy, detailed, extremely cautious. The ship, the reason it was there, what it was for, all this would have to be investigated. The powers that be would monitor it carefully and be ready to respond violently to any threat. An in-loco examination would be necessary before the aliens were allowed onto the Earth's surface. The ship's chemistry would be analysed as well as the biochemistry of its crew. Poisonous chemicals, microorganisms, radioactive emissions, psychic influences, weapons, feeding and hygienic habits, maintenance equipment... All these things and more, would be gone over with a fine toothcomb, before they would even remotely consider allowing the aliens to set foot on Earth.

Maybe they were just so far advanced that they had obtained all the necessary information about them without the need for satellites? Maybe they thought them so insignificant and weak that they only considered them worthy of an informal reception, without pomp or circumstance of any kind? Or maybe they simply had different customs and traditions? Jim Dawson's problem was that he didn't know and had no way of finding out. If there had been lengthy contacts, he would have had time to investigate. This way he had nothing to go on.

"I agree. They can't be that backward. They may even be far more advanced than we are, although their planet doesn't suggest a particularly industrialised civilisation. Nevertheless, Commander, we have many doubts. This is the first large-scale mission aimed at making contact with other civilisations. We have no idea what awaits us, but I'm glad that there really is intelligent life in the Universe! Who knows? Maybe there's a lot they can teach us. The only thing we know for certain is that they have chosen to welcome us."

"Very well, Jim. We'll take the necessary precautions but we'll go by the book. We'll go down there, well intentioned, but we'll be on the look out. We'll convey greetings from the government of the United States and from Earth, and share our joy at making contact with other intelligent beings. I'm glad we've finally made contact with another civilisation, too. We'll symbolically present them with a few samples of some of our most precious goods. But we'll have our fighters on stand-by and, as they've said nothing to the contrary, we'll have our hand lasers with us."

The Commander turned to the central intercom.

"This is the Commander of Star 1, Hamilton Burns, speaking. It is now 16:00 hours on February 5th, 2012. We are currently in orbit around a planet that has identified itself as Ixnor. We have little data on the civilisation we are about to physically make contact with, but are hoping for the best. I trust you are all fully aware of the importance of this event for Earth. I should like to extend my warmest greetings to all the military and civilian representatives of the countries taking part in this mission and hope that you may reap both the material and cultural benefits made possible by it. This is, without a shadow of a doubt, the greatest step mankind has ever taken. Now that our home planet has been fully explored and exploited, we stand on the threshold of a new adventure, a human adventure of unprecedented dimension. We hope to walk away from this first encounter with benefits for all having left a positive image of our planet.

As you know, we have been authorised, invited, to take part in a meeting of representatives. Although the risks involved are considerable, we have decided to accept the invitation. We shall take the Finder 3 exploration vessel. I accept personal responsibility for both this encounter and this mission. As always, should it prove necessary, my replacement has been provided for. We are counting on your determination and goodwill."

Hamilton Burns sat back in his seat. Half closing his eyes, he recalled the events that had led up to this journey. It had all begun in 2003. One November evening, a small alien craft had approached Earth. It remained at a respectable distance for a few days while its crew tried to establish radio contact. An initial brief contact had been made with several of Earth's leaders, sufficient for the latter to let them know that they did not want an immediate physical approach and that further study on how such an approach could be made was necessary. Meanwhile, the intelligence services of various armies attempted to find out as much as they could about the ship and its crew. There was co-operation between various countries to this end, but rivalry on the part of others. The first country to establish a platform of understanding with the aliens would reap tremendous rewards...

So, for reasons which have never been fully explained, the accident happened: the apparently defenceless and almost non-operational ship was hit by a fragment of space refuse (one of the numerous satellites abandoned in orbit) and, not long afterwards, fell to earth. The vessel came down on American soil, thus allowing the United States to head the subsequent research. After a cautious and gradual approach to the crash site, it was concluded that neither the ship nor the dead crew represented any danger to Humanity. On the contrary, the gains were extraordinary: the secrets of space translocation were unlocked.

The ordinary inhabitants of the planet were only told about this top-secret close encounter several months after the event. However, when the story finally broke, it was accompanied by a piece of news which shook public opinion and the media around the world, and over the following months dominated it: thanks to the initial radio contacts with the alien vessel (which had produced a basic alien-human dictionary), multi-national researchers had been able to decipher documents found amongst the wreckage of the spaceship. The documents, which were not as yet fully understood, were essentially comprised of schematic diagrams and drawings, and explained how to construct a spaceship capable of traversing immeasurable distances almost instantaneously. The earthmen suddenly found themselves in possession of the technology necessary for exploration not only of the solar system but also of places thousands of light-years away. This led to a storm of speculation in numerous circles, not only scientific and military but also journalistic, philosophical, religious and biological. What were the true implications? What did the possibility of being able to travel anywhere in the Universe really mean to Humanity? What were the advantages and risks involved? To what extent was man going beyond his own biological limits? By adopting an alien technology that he did not master or fully comprehend, would man be taking risks which were as yet incalculable? Could this not result in unsuspected dangers to the planet? By betraying their presence and giving away their location, might they not be attracting the aggression of more advanced peoples? And as the aliens had been able to master translocation and the laws of energy and matter inherent in it, was it not possible that they also possessed unimaginably destructive weapons? If they were capable of instantly materialising in Earth's orbit, could they not do this undetected and conquer the planet? Or perhaps this was not the case. Perhaps this was a real chance to make hitherto impossible advances in medicine, psychology, art. And besides, it would be feasible to transport valuable material and biological resources of great benefit for mankind from afar.

Hamilton Burns had closely followed the initial contacts and experiments during 2007. He had, in fact, been one of the project supervisors. The first two attempts had gone catastrophically wrong: the first had simply resulted in the disintegration of the ship and its crew of volunteers; in the second, the vessel had totally disappeared. The problem apparently lay in the use of plastics, which were later abolished as one of the "wizards" (as he tended to think of the specialists in meditation consulted by the Air Force) claimed that these "muffled" the "vibrations of the natural world" and would thus not provide the necessary resonance. It was also possible that the first navigators had been badly selected and, as a result of their poor powers of concentration, had been incapable of summing up the correct psychic state necessary for translocation. All subsequent attempts had proved extremely successful, however. An experimental ship had actually approached Aldebaran but returned with a crew of just three men - one of which was a monk specialising in astrophysics. From the initial research to construction of the space cruiser "Star 1" was just one step. An extraordinarily expensive step, but one considered politically unavoidable: the United States had to take it if they wanted to maintain their comfortable supremacy in space exploration. And so, in October 2012, Hamilton Burns was officially awarded command of a spaceship heading for the area where, according to the logs found on board the alien spacecraft which had crashed on American soil, there was a planet inhabited by intelligent human beings.

Chapter 3

Deliberation

All was well on Ixnor. With the dawn of a new day, the planet's great white sun began another cycle that would ensure the physical wellbeing of a naturally lush and peaceful world. Animals and human beings alike responded gratefully to its soft light as they began to stir. Throughout the small towns of stone, metal and wooden houses, the inhabitants were beginning another productive and contemplative day. For many Ixnorians, this meant little more than taking care of the natural world. On Earth, they might be taken for gardeners and farmers, ecologists, biologists and other specialists - were it not for the ceremonial, almost devotional way in which they approached their work, with both mobile and immobile things, and the utter joy with which they carried it out. They were often seen waving a friendly hello to large trees, or sitting still for long periods at a time, their eyes closed, next to a stone corner or a patch of vegetables with which they felt a particular bio-magnetic affinity. They would then reflect on the impressions they had gained from their intimate contact with animals, vegetables and minerals - or with the numerous energy-filled beings which ran these settlements. The result was, that even the simplest tasks were carried out with abundant creativity and a sense of togetherness by those who consciously shared cosmic life. Indeed, for the more "aware" Ixnorians, the planet itself was not seen as a limitation: it was merely a point of support and exteriorisation for a psychological life, which included not only the kingdoms of nature, but extraplanetary cosmic kingdoms too. Its inner world was in tune with the Universe, the "Land of Unlimited Space", providing limitless possibilities. "What is inside is the same as what is outside. What is above is the same as what is below. Everything is analogous. Everything is in tune." And they were intensely free and peaceful.

Other inhabitants of the planet took care of what was produced or transformed by the human hand. These were the equivalent of Earth engineers, architects, artists, craftsmen, teachers, scientists and other conveyors or producers of culture and civilisation. Some created artefacts of all sizes and shapes, from great engineering and architectural works to individual designs or the recording of knowledge, in materials ranging from crystal to wood or laminated metal; others created pedagogical aids, undertook scientific research or provided other varied contributions to civilised living.

Ixnor had the look of an untamed world, only slightly transformed by the activity of intelligent beings. In fact, these made a point of keeping it this way, and many of their great engineering or architectural works had made large use of naturally existing contours. For this reason, many of their dwellings and buildings blended in with the surrounding terrain and, as they were constructed of locally extracted materials, were almost invisible from the air. The Ixnorians sought to live in harmony with objects, places and living beings and, whenever possible, accentuate this congruence. That was the supreme objective of Art. As for Science, it aimed to provide the inhabitants of the planet with the knowledge of all things micro and macrocosmic, internal and external. Indeed, for the Ixnorians, the notion of frontiers between the various conceptual and physical limits was relative. It was merely another instrument for the activity of life. And this was greeted and respected wherever it was found, not out of duty but out of understanding and intimate contact with it. For a human inhabitant of Ixnor, even a small bird deserved to be treated carefully and respectfully, the spontaneous simplicity with which this occurred notwithstanding.

One day, a giant Earth ship materialised in orbit above Ixnor: just another of the many ships which visited the planet, although unusually large.

The Central Council always met on such occasions. This was more of a courtesy measure than an absolute necessity, since interplanetary or interstellar relations had for many centuries been part of normal life on Ixnor. The inhabitants hated routine, however, and would never consider other living beings as unworthy of their full attention. Besides, these visitors were as yet unknown and were probably bringing with them an opportunity for mutual cultural enrichment.

Beneath the transparent dome at the centre of the Crystal Star, Axor, the planet leader, rang the Bell of Light with the Sceptre of Humility. The crystalline sound rang out through the whole building as the various members of the Planetary Council adopted an attitude of inner contemplation, using the vibrations of the building to help deepen their state of meditation still further. As the air vibrated around them, their bodies and minds resonated in harmony with the sound of the bell, molecules and organs slipping into a state of heightened awareness. Within, their sensations, feelings and thoughts took on an increasingly deeper rhythmic empathy, reaching an apex of equilibrium many octaves higher. Their minds also tuned in, mutually strengthening each other in the search for greater clarity and balance, while in gentle tones Axor summarised the theme of joint contemplation. The very sound of this voice was part of the vibration, seeming to reach down into the deepest core of those present and there awaken the highest level of human competence.

"Brothers, you all know that at this precise moment a giant spaceship carrying about 5000 human souls is orbiting Ixnor. They have come from a distant planet and, as you also know, according to our tradition we have abstained from scanning them. Nevertheless," - and at this moment Axor's voice took on a slightly foreboding tone - "the vibrations of the crew appear surprisingly obscure. It appears that, for reasons we cannot as yet fathom, a group unable to exteriorise its inner conscience has approached us. This leads us to conclude that we should analyse events extremely carefully. The Rule of Welcome requires that we receive them in a fitting manner. Should there be no objections, I propose that Gael receives them on the Norya plateau."

For a few moments silence prevailed, while inside the crystal dome the inner sound vibrated in all its subtleties. The united minds pondered. Then Liriel, the Watcher of the Council, spoke her thoughts.

"I am in agreement with Axor's words, but wish to add another detail. The ship which has approached us reveals the presence of instruments of generalised destruction. Although we must abstain from judging the intentions of these people, we must take this into consideration. I suggest we adopt an attitude of benevolent supervision."

The meeting moved on to discussion of other important issues pertinent to planetary development. Odeon, the officiant for Climatic Management, presented ecological data indicating the usefulness of carrying out a slow and gentle increase in average daily rainfall in the third zone of Ixnor's southern hemisphere. Aila, the officiant of Ethics, announced that the population in general had reported a continued favourable evolution in the serenity and spiritual alignment with the Purpose of the local solar system. Inner freedom continued to be enjoyed by all and joyful living was at its highest level throughout the planet. No crime had been committed on Ixnor for 557 years.

The meeting culminated in prolonged irradiation from the Constructive Light. The shared conscience of the Council absorbed the influence of Ixnor's sun and other distant stars. According to the ancient Ixnorian saying, it "received the grace of the stars", then "reverberating with the fabric of the Universe" touched the energy core of the planet, evoking a powerful activating response from, and then channelling of, the subtle "fire" accumulated there. The Crystal Star, the complex translucent building, at whose heart lay the Dome of Unification, began to vibrate rhythmically, responding to the energy at the planet's core and exteriorising it. At each synchronised breath of the members of the Council, the exhaled sound of communion caused the crystal to pulsate deeply expanding energy. At that moment all the human beings on Ixnor knew within that the Planetary Council was blessing them. Their simple response spread throughout the planet's "network of conscious light", which in turn sparkled and glittered in multi-coloured hues. And simultaneously, at other points of energy somewhere in the vastness of space, on other worlds, there was an answering echo and the Symphony of Cosmic Life became more complete.

A little later, in a different place, Axor went peacefully about his usual daily gardening tasks, whilst Liriel and Gael chatted about the best way of making their food plants grow and develop. At their usual places, the inhabitants of the planet were already aware of the decisions that had been taken and carried them out calmly, jointly, efficiently. Should anyone not agree with the decisions taken, they could opt either not to execute them or to talk to the leaders about them. Each inhabitant was allowed his or her say, and could even take part in meetings of the

Council, although this rarely occurred: the leaders of Ixnor were aware of the needs of the inhabitants of the planet and did their best to find a middle point between these needs and the Purpose of the Solar System of which they were a part. They were generally able to accomplish this in a balanced and satisfactory manner. In a way, the governing of Ixnor was the result of a permanent psychic referendum.

Chapter 4

Selection

For some time, American Air Force Intelligence had been frantically searching for candidates. They scoured yoga academies, esoteric schools, monasteries and universities. Those selected had to have impeccable backgrounds, be in good physical condition, enjoy good health and, above all, have an in-depth knowledge of meditation and techniques of self-control. Ideally they would be single and have few emotional ties on Earth, as eventually they would be offered the chance of travelling unimaginable distances without the possibility of contacting Earth or even any guarantee of ever returning to it. They could not be troublemakers nor sympathetic to international political forces opposed to space travel. There were no restrictions as to gender, but in the case of female candidates it was absolutely imperative that they not be pregnant; they also had to solemnly undertake that they would not become pregnant either during the selection and training process or later during the mission itself. A pregnancy could alter their ability to concentrate and render them unfit for the mission objectives - this was, at least, what the military feared. They should also have a sound cultural background and be fluent in more than one language. The mission would probably be a multinational one and would imply contact with alien beings whose linguistic subtleties were as of yet unknown.

On 8 December 2010, General Katie Forster called a meeting with the heads of intelligence. She was not overly pleased with the progress of events and went straight to the point.

"Gentleman, I have carefully gone over the files of the candidates and, generally speaking, am greatly disappointed. It seems that most of them are one sandwich short of a picnic. Their dress sense is worse than their character, and they have led very irregular lives. Do you plan on sending a lunatic to Ursa Major or wherever the hell it is we're going?"

Jordan Lansing, the head of intelligence, had been expecting the outburst. He had known Kate for many years and although he didn't particularly like the wilful nature of this short, stocky woman, he recognised some good qualities in her. One of these was the frank manner in which she dealt with people.

"Unfortunately there does seem to be a connection between intense meditation and the adoption of, let's say, rather eccentric ideas and ways of life. Unless, of course, it's the eccentric ones that are most attracted to meditation. I wouldn't give most of these candidates a second look. "

"Jordan, you know very well that I don't call meetings for the fun of it. I presume you have formed an opinion as to those best suited?"

"Yes, I have, general. If you look closely, you'll notice that three files have small red marks on them. I believe that those three contain the three most likely candidates."

Katie Forster quickly leafed through the three files. Linda Beauchamp, a graduate in Engineering. 36 years old. Married with no children. Residing in a house on the outskirts of New York. Clean background. Excellent medical history. Had practised Transcendental Meditation for 10 years and presently taught it. Knowledgeable in other forms of meditation. Ross Wentworth, graduate in Agronomy. 43 years old. Excellent medical history. Manager of an alternative agriculture farm in Kansas. Married with no children. Had demonstrated against the Arab-American War of 2001. Currently ran a Tibetan Yoga school. Henry Livingstone, a Doctor of Philosophy. 50 years old. Single. Keen on martial arts. Excellent medical history. Supporter of ecological methods. Experienced oriental philosophy conference speaker. Raja and Agni Yoga instructor.

Katie moved the files to one side and looked at the director of intelligence. These three did seem the best choice. Even their photographs were more convincing than the others, most of which were of people with shaved heads and purple tunics, or covered in hair and wearing very few clothes.

"At first sight, Jordan, I have to agree with you. We need to tread carefully, though. I presume that psychological tests were run on these three?"

"Certainly. And they all seem to fit the bill. Honest people. Seem to have handled themselves very well in the past in stressful situations. Independent types, achievers, able to make quick decisions under stress. None of them has a criminal record and all wish to be of service to society. And that could be important if we decide to take them on. Money doesn't mean much to them - two of them could be earning three times as much if they wanted to."

"No military experience?"

"Unfortunately not. I'm afraid we'll be dealing with fairly staunch pacifists."

"Well, we won't be giving too much away about the ship's military capabilities anyway. They'll just concentrate on their role as navigators and, of course, it'll be important to motivate them according to their own personal interests."

"Do I take it you plan to call the three of them?"

"Yes, the three of them. We'll see how things go, then select one of them, perhaps a second to act as a stand-in. As you know, we've already selected other people - those involved in the first phase of the Stellar Way project. We can rely on them if necessary but we'd prefer to leave our options open."

Four months later, General Forster met in private with Jordan.

"Right. Let's discuss this man you've chosen. I've had a chance to talk to him. He seems pleasant enough but seems to keep his thoughts to himself. The results of his tests and training were excellent; it appears we've found our navigator. Commander Burns has a reasonable opinion of the man. Even so, I'd still like to hear your opinion. Can we trust the guy? "

"That's just the problem. I'm convinced he'd stand up to interrogation just as well as any of my top agents. Besides, he's asked various questions about the objectives of his mission and the reason why we'll be carrying nuclear weaponry. The first time he asked we hadn't even briefed him."

"You mean that he's been prying around or that he obtained the information by paranormal means? What is he, some sort of sorcerer?"

"Apparently. Mind you, it's fairly obvious we wouldn't go traversing the universe unarmed. Besides, he could have been trying to test us."

"I'd deduce as much myself. But from the look on your face, I'd say you're not entirely convinced?"

"He's a strange man. A few days ago he was exhausted. Then a vidcall was put through to the base and the operator asked him if he wanted to take it. It was a friend of his who was worried about some perfectly mundane issue and had rung him at home. In his place, I'd have told the operator to say I wasn't in. But the guy just said he "didn't believe in lying" and was on the phone with his friend for ages. Naturally we taped the whole thing. Everyday chitchat with some spiritual advice on yoga meditation thrown in. After he'd hung up, our Henry Livingstone seemed a lot less tired than before the call."

"He recovered from his exhaustion while speaking on the telephone?"

"Yep. He claims that, "when friends are in need, we can always find a little bit more of ourselves to give". But what really worries me is this feeling that the guy's motives are unclear. When you ask him how he feels about going on an interstellar journey, he usually says something like, "it's just another step towards returning to the unity of things". He never mentions money or fame or future interests. He is totally committed to his training though, and seems determined to ensure that nothing can go wrong."

"And? Wasn't that what we wanted?"

"Yes, it was. But if ever a time comes when we need to use force out there, I'm afraid he won't take it very well."

"You think he might side with the aliens? That doesn't make any sense. He seems to show great loyalty, patriotism even. Don't you think?"

"True enough. But you know me. In intelligence, we don't like people who can't be read if they don't want to be - unless they're one of us and we have good reasons for believing them loyal. And this character is one of those."

"...As long as you don't give him too much information, I don't really see the problem. Which version of the mission objective have you given him?"

"Only what we agreed upon. That the possibility that we might be able to establish a colony, justified the ship's size and a crew of five thousand. We stressed that the weapons were only there for self-defence and gave him no details on them. We told him as little as possible about the possibility of harvesting large quantities of minerals and vegetable and animal specimens or how the mission would be paid. We obviously didn't mention the fact that we'd like to run a few biochemical and psychological tests on at least one of the alien locals. We're not even sure we're going to make contact with intelligent beings."

"Excellent. Keep him keen if you can and only give him information on a need-to-know basis. But make sure that what you do tell him is said in such a way as to make him believe there's nothing else to know. As for the rest, make sure that there are others on board who can take Livingstone's place if need be. Has that been taken care of?"

"Of course. There are various meditation students from different schools among the crew. We believe we can count on them should anything untoward befall Livingstone. In fact, our friend has agreed to produce a training manual, and has almost completed it. There are also two crew members who could easily take his place, although they do seem slightly less qualified: one of the men who took part in Stellar Way is an engineer called Martinez, and an officer called Diana Goodwin."

A little while later, Jordan Lansing found himself alone in his office. If it weren't for the fact that he was going on sixty, had a family and, quite naturally, felt a certain foreboding, he too would very much like to travel on the ship. Those going on the journey would have a unique experience and be welcomed as heroes on their return. They might even be acclaimed as the providers of fabulous wealth. The records found on board the wrecked alien ship pointed to amazing riches in the subsoil of the planet New Hope. There didn't really seem much chance of serious difficulties arising. There were no signs of any weapons on board the ship nor was there any mention of them on New Hope. The Earth ship was carrying enough armament to obliterate several planets and Commander Burns was a military leader with a proven track record. On board were a variety of military and civilian specialists as well as state-of-the-art physical, chemical, biochemical, neurological and psychological research equipment. Any events would have to be documented and detailed over a period of many years and they had the suitable equipment to do it with. There were a large number of conventionally propelled craft, land and aquatic vehicles on board armed with laser, sonic and chemical weapons. Even the construction materials and tools had been adapted to allow for the fast erection of large buildings if necessary. Everything had been thought out down to the smallest technical detail. If he were just a few years younger...

Chapter 5

The Navigator

Henry Livingstone could hardly believe what was happening. His childhood dream of making contact with extraterrestrials - whom he had never been able to imagine as slimy threatening monsters - was now coming true. Already they were orbiting the planet New Hope and a few hours from now would be coming into contact with a different civilisation for the first time. Unlike his fellow crewmembers, Henry Livingstone did not regard this moment with the slightest apprehension. By concentrating inwardly he found an irresistible empathy with this new world, one whose vibratory influence was remarkable. It was at once overwhelming yet absolutely invigorating, and gave him a feeling of strength, purity and constructive energy. Livingstone looked forward to forming a bond of friendship with beings, which he felt inside, were probably more in tune with his nature than the majority of his fellow Earthmen. But these emotions could not disguise the anguish that had been building inside him over the last few days. Sitting with his legs crossed, the navigator's mind wandered over the events which had brought him so far from Earth...

On a January day in 2001, Livingstone was sitting comfortably at home in Vermont, reading Thoreau's "Walden", when he heard a knock at the door. Wearing his old dressing gown, he got up and walked towards it. Two men in Air Force uniforms stood outside, a look of curiosity and surprise on their faces. He too was astonished at finding neatly turned out military uniforms - instead of woodcutters, for example - at his front door.

"Good morning. Doctor Henry Livingstone?" asked one of them. "My name is Bradley and this is my aide, Atkinson. We'd like a word with you if possible, sir."

"Certainly. Please come in."

Livingstone was curious. He had never had any dealings with the Air Force before. What on earth could they want with him? However, he was one of those men that still believed in the importance of hospitality. The two officers calmly accepted the invitation to sit down.

"We'll come straight to the point", Bradley said with a smile. "Have you been following the news about the possibility of interstellar travel?"

"I certainly have. The subject fascinates me, particularly as it seems that the knowledge that would make it possible is extraterrestrial."

"But I am sure you are unaware, as the general public are, that such journeys are only possible through the direct intervention of the human mind?"

"What do you mean?" Livingstone was becoming more interested in this visit by the minute...

"I must warn you that anything we tell you from this moment on must be regarded as highly confidential. The personal consequences to yourself would be rather unpleasant should you disclose any secrets."

Livingstone did not like the warning tone implicit in this last sentence. He would have preferred it if they had simply asked him to keep a secret. It would have been far more polite, and had he been asked to give his word, he would not have broken it under any circumstances. He was only too well aware, however, that he lived in a paranoid world where distrust and betrayal were the yardstick against which most human relationships are measured...

"May I ask why you should wish to reveal state secrets to me?"

Bradley's answer was immediate. He seemed to have rehearsed what he was about to say, delighting in the effect that his words would have.

"Because, Dr. Livingstone, we are interested in your services for a hypothetical interstellar journey."

The effect was evident. Despite his many years of training in abstraction and self-control, Livingstone could hardly believe his ears. His expression must have been a cross between amazement and disbelief.

"My services? But I know almost nothing about aeronautics, physics, mathematics, or whatever it is an expert in such matters is supposed to know. I'm not even a very good driver. My interests are more philosophical, the search for knowledge and..."

"Precisely. And you're wrong in that respect. As I said before, the human element is essential. Only someone with a profound understanding of the art of meditation can translocate through space."

"Translocate? Would you be kind enough to explain what on earth you're talking about?"

"Can we count on absolute discretion on your part as to what we are about to reveal?"

"Yes of course. I give you my word that I will not reveal anything to anyone."

Livingstone was enjoying finding himself attentively following a conversation which seemed to have come straight out of a science fiction novel. Nevertheless, the people sitting here in front of him obviously took very seriously what they had come all this way to tell him, and they certainly didn't appear to be insane. A little neurotic perhaps, but insane... no. Could it be that, for some reason he hadn't yet fathomed, the age-old science of meditation and inner contemplation had joined forces with state-of-the-art astronautic technology?

"Basically what we are dealing with is the possibility of instantaneously transporting huge masses across immeasurable distances."

"And that's where the human element comes in?"

"Exactly. There are mechanisms by which an entire spaceship can be placed in synchronisation with the human mind in such a way that, should the person be sufficiently skilled, it can be transported instantly to a place with which it has been synched. The experiment has already been successfully carried out. But a human element with unquestionable mental powers and training is fundamental."

Henry Livingstone was fascinated. His childhood memories and adult speculations were being reawakened - and it all made perfect sense to someone who believed that, inevitably, there had to be some connection between what he read in books on quantum physics and what he knew and experienced in the world of Transpersonal Psychology and the mystical and esoteric traditions of the whole planet. In fact, it was all rather reminiscent of the journeys of the Shamans.

"And... and is that why you're here?"

"Indeed", said Atkinson. "And we've done our homework. We know that you are regarded as rather an authority on the theory and practice of meditation. Your disciples say that neither your abilities nor your honesty should be questioned. What we need is a specialist like you. He must also be trustworthy, loyal, and preferably with few or no family ties. It is difficult to assess the extent of the risks involved."

Taking risks did not bother Livingstone if, of course, he thought it was worth it - and to decide whether it was worth it, he would not consider any immediate personal gain but rather how many people might benefit, and to what extent, should he decide to risk his life.

"What do you expect of me?"

"That you accept our invitation and, in a few hours, accompany us to a secret destination. You will move in there, should you accept. You will receive a salary far higher than your present one and excellent perks. Besides - and we know how important this is to you - you will have a unique opportunity to help mankind."

And that was how it all began. One month later, he had acquired the habit of getting up early in the morning at a military base, the exact location of which he did not know, to undergo psychological, neurological and biochemical tests, attend physical training sessions and meetings with senior state and military officials. These officials seemed to have suddenly developed an interest in Perene Philosophy and classical meditation techniques, not to mention oriental traditions. However, he was under no illusions: not one of them had captured the spirit of the thing. Their only interest was in the technical possibilities and they viewed meditation as a special means of placing the human brain in the correct electroencephalographic rhythm or allowing "something connected with energy", as yet not catalogued and quantified and which they referred to as the "T factor", to act. Metaphysics meant nothing to them nor did they show the slightest interest in the meaning of existence or discovering whether or not they possessed a soul. They had simply been forced to admit that the occupants of the alien spaceship which had crashed on Earth, knew how to travel instantaneously across the galaxies by entering a state of meditation. In fact, the alien beings found dead inside the ship were similar to ordinary human beings, the only difference being that their organisms were unpolluted and their pineal glands were slightly larger.

Sadly, Livingstone realised that the military were solely interested in him because he knew how to place himself into an altered state of awareness - and also, perhaps, because he knew how to train people to do the same. His own ideas about the reasons underlying meditation were of little interest to them.

The navigator took advantage of the moment to try and pinpoint the source of his anguish. Who was he after all? "Just a man trying to become whole", his inner self seemed to reply. In fact, that's what he seemed to have been doing all his life. For as long as he could remember, he had always tried to understand and explore the potential of human beings and, of course, his own. In his youth he had studied theatre, martial arts, the cinema, gymnastics, yoga and philosophy. For a long time now he had dedicated himself to meditation, attempting ever-higher levels of increased inward purity, greater capacity for discretion, detachment and abstraction. He was searching for illumination, trying to attain a state where he had a clear and total vision "of the World in its intimacy and in its reality", as he liked to think. And on the path to achieving his objective, he found it best to adopt an ethical approach and benevolent attitude to those around him. How could he achieve total understanding of reality and human beings if there were areas of learning and contact, or human possibilities, which he a priori rejected? Would it be possible to tune into the whole of humanity if he refused to recognise or admit in himself all the possibilities of human expression, from the most vile to the most noble feelings, from the greatest selfishness to the greatest self-denial? He had chosen a constructive route but not because the others were unfamiliar to him. To Livingstone it seemed obvious that in order to understand a murderer, you should be able to feel that part of yourself, which, with the "right" amount of distortion or exaggeration, would make you a murderer.

Nevertheless, to those that knew him, he was nothing short of a holy man. Some of his friends went as far as to ask him, jokingly, whether he shouldn't be living in a cave in India instead, wearing a loincloth and a turban. But Livingstone had a relatively western appearance. At the age of fifty, with a smooth unlined face, a man that dressed in a rather moderate manner "to avoid being noticed", with a thin and muscular build as a result of regular physical exercise, he did not resemble the stereotype usually associated with oriental gurus. His black hair and brown eyes did not give him a completely American look either. There were also those who believed that at the end of the fifth decade of his life, the look in his eyes and the smile on his face still gave him the air of a curious, fascinated child.

The navigator suddenly realised he had been letting his mind wander, but he didn't ignore the curious path down which it had wandered. Perhaps the anguish he felt was somehow related. By concentrating, he concluded that it was.

He had just translocated a gigantic spaceship and its heavily armed crew. Many of them were experienced soldiers who had already had the chance - and for them, the need - to kill other human beings and had actually gone through with it. Many of them were capable of identifying with violence without inwardly possessing the ability to counterbalance this aspect of their natures. Many of them were extremely disciplined but, it seemed, ethics were not their strong point. They probably would never even have considered what kind of behaviour would be deemed correct on space voyages and in interplanetary or interstellar contacts.

Feeling a knot of anguish in the pit of his stomach, Livingstone suddenly remembered that the ship was carrying a considerable number of nuclear weapons. He had been assured by the highest ranking military officers that these were strictly for self-defence. Now, however, a flash of insight had increased his anguish even further. Could he really believe that such weapons of mass destruction were primarily for defensive purposes? Perhaps it was the old "dissuasion through terror" tactic: whoever they encountered would fear being totally wiped out and would thus not dare to attack them. But the mere presence of such weapons indicated an attitude of savage mistrust. Besides, the navigator could not rely on the judgement of the military or even the on-board civilian observers to determine where and when they would have the right to consider themselves as under attack, to the extent where they would be justified in using nuclear weapons. Particularly because they were among a "strange" people, which may lead to the adoption of the less noble scruples with which, centuries before, European explorers had treated entire races in what was then known as the New World.

Frightened and embarrassed, Livingstone realised that he had just translocated a spaceship peopled with excellent representatives of a paranoid and ethically handicapped culture. He had allowed himself to be tempted by the prospect of the journey and by his blind faith in the good intentions of his fellow beings. Now all he could do was wait and try, as best he could, to prevent events snowballing towards disaster...

Chapter 6

The Journey

The synthesised musical alarm sounded throughout the huge orbiting ship. Translocation was scheduled to take place shortly. Despite the immeasurable distance, this enormous vessel was about to travel instantaneously from its current position above the Earth to a place in orbit around the planet known as "New Hope". Even though they had been carefully selected and trained, the state of mind of the crew at their different posts shifted as they heard the alarm from confident calmness to extreme unease. They were aware that from this point on their destiny was in the hands of a single man and his psychic abilities. They also knew that, within the next few minutes, they should either fall into a deep, perhaps chemically induced sleep, or a state of profound relaxation. Their minds should relax and their emotions focus on the success of the journey; their bodies should become limp, the muscles fully relaxed. Otherwise, sleep would be preferable. In the meantime, individual monitors checked the brain patterns of each man or woman so that when translocation took place no brain would be too active. Should this occur, the on-board computer would locate the individual and an alarm would alert him or her of the need to take a fast-acting sleep inducer; the navigator would also be warned to delay the departure for several minutes.

At his command post, Hamilton Burns sought to obey the pre-launch procedure despite the fact that it went profoundly against his nature. If he were ordered to pilot a fighter, he would be in his element; if he were given orders to make some delicate decision, he would easily carry them out. Yet what they were asking him to do was simply take a deep breath, relax his body and let his thoughts wander as if on the edge of dream - this if he could not simply "reach a state of mental void". It was almost too much for someone who had always considered himself a man of action. "Relax while someone else instantly takes you on an impossible journey to the stars", he thought semi-sarcastically. "Let all your worries drift away whilst the greatest financial investment in the history of mankind travels thousands of light years in the wink of an eye and all you get to do is relax". Irritated, Burns concluded that when all was said and done, he would not be able quickly and consciously to place his brain in a stable alpha rhythm, or perhaps theta-delta, as was apparently ideal. Despite his training - the same training received by all those on the ship - he preferred not to risk becoming a hindrance or hearing the alarm go off and seeing the warning light come on, humiliatingly indicating to the whole crew that their commanding officer could not attain the "whatever-it-was-required-degree-of-meditation" and needed to take a hypno-inducer. He felt helpless and, however hard he tried not to admit it, distinctly apprehensive as he took the pill.

Livingstone sat comfortably in the navigation centre of the huge ship. He turned the lighting down to a pleasant softness and calmly lit an incense stick. As he did, he gently poked fun at himself: there he was, the man responsible for translocating the gigantic "Star 1" with all its on-board personnel and technical apparatus - something like five thousand men and women, a billion tons of metal, supplies, machinery and, unfortunately, weapons - lighting a small stick of incense before concentrating... The habit was, however, a long-standing one and either through conditioned reflex or ritualistic symbology, or both, the smell of the incense helped him to attain a profound state of abstraction - one that had nothing to do with his nose. His light-hearted nature, though, the fact that he did not take himself particularly seriously as a human being, made concentrating that much easier and prevented him from being overwhelmed by the sense of responsibility.

As the smoke drifted slowly through the navigation deck, Livingstone unravelled the chart showing the location in the galaxy of the planet, which (if the indications found in the small alien craft that had had the misfortune to crash on Earth were accurate) they were to visit. He thought to himself: "All places are familiar to the Spirit". This was no cliché. He really believed it and it had been one of the reasons he had been chosen. And anyway, the possibility that a human being could tune in "live" to a distant point in the Universe was a mystery in itself. Not "tuning" as we now know it, as this would imply receiving electromagnetic waves and these would be little more than vibrating fossils after the thousands of light years they had travelled. In fact, the term "tuning" was inappropriate, since this was not about receiving waves - unless they moved at an infinite velocity or could "leap" billions and billions of kilometres - and yet it appeared that certain humans could travel beyond space and time and somehow "relate" with events taking place simultaneously thousands of light years away.

Checking his monitor to see how near the members of the crew were to attaining the required brain pattern, the navigator activated the first command. Instants later, he began to feel the first pleasant effects of the electromagnetic field that would increase his biopsychic harmony, simultaneously affecting his central nervous and vegetative system and enhancing his nerve cells. He closed his eyes, relaxing his eyelids, and concentrated on placing his neural functions into a qualitatively and quantitatively heightened state at the increasingly slower rhythm of the soft sound waves synchronised with the pulse of the electromagnetic field. He blocked out the thought and sense of responsibility of having thousands of lives in his hands at that instant; he blocked out the fear of not returning, of failing, of getting lost. He blocked out all sources of emotional and mental stress, all diversions, anything that might distract his senses. He concentrated solely on the inner flow towards the objective. Then, as his state of relaxation and mental abstraction deepened, he reviewed the data he had on their point of destination and its characteristics. Using his creative imagination, he pictured a luminous band between his home planet and (traversing the parsecs, many times 19 billion miles) the planet known for the time being as "New Hope". Moments earlier, the monitor had indicated that all the ship's crew were reaching the required minimum brain pattern. So Livingstone activated the second command.

The resonators scattered around the ship went into action, bombarding animate and inanimate structures with sound waves and ultra-sound waves, setting up a reverberating eco-tuning vibration. This beat out a basic, uniform rhythm, which kept the ship and crew in a vibratory state of stable oscillation. A few seconds later, sound waves controlled by the navigator's brain rhythms, monitored via a sophisticated form of tele-electroencephalography, added a melodic variation to the basic sound rhythm. In a sense, each nook and cranny of the enormous metallic structure was being tuned by the navigator's brain and - for those who believed in it - by something else, the "T factor". The whole ship, the geometric forms and materials of which had been designed in such a way as to increase vibration, began to resonate subtly. Men and animals, asleep or fully relaxed, plants, machinery, all and any molecular structure, obeyed the vibratory patterns transmitted by the resonators. The whole ship - circular in structure like a gigantic flying saucer - was ready for the journey, if you could call an instantaneous change in spatial co-ordinates a journey?

Livingstone fell deeper into meditation, into a profoundly altered state of consciousness, and focused on his own subatomic level. He concentrated on the vibration of the particles and their response to the eco-tuning pattern. He then expanded his awareness until he felt all the subatomic particles of the ship vibrating in unison. The ship was a whole and he was a part of that whole, there and now. He and the ship, with all its inhabitants, was a continuity that vibrated... At that moment, the reality of love as energy was the playing field of his consciousness. A uniform, free playing field between the infinitely large and the infinitely small, between the near and the far. A playing field far beyond space and time... Then, instead of imagining the whole of the me-ship at another point in space, the navigator felt this point, tuned into it, and deliberately joined with it, ignoring time and distance. With all his willpower, he "felt" the me-ship in the place in space into which he had tuned. There was something akin to a flash, an explosion of light inside him and inside everything on the ship. At that precise moment, a huge vessel materialised above the planet Ixnor. Translocation was complete, contact about to be made.

The navigator consciously "fixed" the vibrating structure at the new point in space, the orbit around the planet that he still knew as "New Hope", and then, slowly, very slowly, without altering his basic brain patterns, shut down the resonators. Next, also emerging slowly and cautiously from his state of meditation, he turned off the electromagnetic field. He breathed deeply, as yet unable to take in as the small being that he once again felt, the idea of what he had just accomplished, and half opened his eyes. Smiling, he checked that his surroundings were still familiar and that, from within, he felt no threat. He stretched like a cat, enjoying the return to a state of normal alertness, whilst he happily realised that everything had gone smoothly and that, all over the ship, numerous people were living the most important events of their lives. He then triggered the command to awaken the senior officers. Soon, the familiar face of Commander Burns appeared on his monitor. He had only just awoken, but already felt fully alert and, of course, in his element. An enthusiastic smile surfaced from under his somewhat hard features.

"Congratulations, Dr. Livingstone. My sincerest congratulations. I have just ascertained that we are not, in any manner of speaking, where we were a few minutes ago. I'd dearly like to know how such a thing is possible, but I'll be damned if it isn't."

"Thank you. I believe that you are in charge now, and to be honest, I've no idea what will happen next. I don't really understand the procedures involved in commanding an object the size of this ship. Request permission to join you?"

"Permission granted. Quite frankly, you deserve one hell of a handshake and to hell with protocol! Mankind shall not forget this day nor the name of the person that made spatial translocation possible. I should tell you that we now know that this planet is inhabited!"

"Thank you, Commander. I shall be right there."

For a few moments, the navigator remained lost in thought. Personal compliments meant little to him. His life had been a succession of acts dictated by his conscience and by the desire to be useful to others. He had accepted the mission because he believed it could prove of great use for all mankind. And anyway, he did not feel overly at ease with Hamilton Burns. He had the feeling that he and the Commander belonged to different worlds. Worlds that were ethically and conceptually different; different ways of feeling and seeing things. It was then, for the first time, that Livingstone felt an inner anguish and the need to find out more about its source...

Chapter 7

The Encounter

Finder 3, the exploration vessel, had just landed noisily in the centre of the Norya plateau. The vessel's solid fuel reactors, which had provided the thrust to move away from Star 1 and enter the Ixnorian atmosphere, stirred up huge gusts of wind and clouds of dust as it approached the planet surface. Gael stood with two other Inxorians a few hundred metres from the landing site as the Earthmen descended the ramp and set foot on the planet for the first time. She was somewhat puzzled: she had expected their vehicle to at least be equipped with an anti-gravity device, and had never imagined it would be so cumbersome, so polluting and noisy. Didn't they realise that the din from the vessel's engines could cause untold damage to the planet's natural environment and its inhabitants? The sound vibrations had an unbalanced, grating quality to them. They should have been aware of such things and yet had failed to warn the Ixnorians about them. It was important not to prejudge the newcomers, however. Although there were reasons to...

Further ahead, Hamilton Burns, Jim Dawson, the navigator Henry Livingstone and a few armed crewmembers looked carefully around. The natural landscape was welcoming and the climate mild, as their instruments had earlier confirmed. The clean, fresh air smelt of trees and flowers while, beneath their feet, semi-transparent rocks reflected the sunlight in astonishing hues of colour, and even appeared to give off their own light. Several brightly coloured birds soared here and there, seemingly unruffled by their presence. Their small size seemed to indicate that they, too, were no threat. From their current position, the humans could only make out the three Ixnorians, standing motionless next to a leafy tree. They headed towards them, the Commander having carefully observed them through his precision binoculars.

They were completely human in appearance: light-skinned with golden brown hair, slender, elegant bodies, five fingers on each hand, similar bodily proportions. It appeared that Mother Nature tended to build human beings of the same physical type even when thousands of light years apart - which, it suddenly occurred to the navigator, might indicate the existence of totally non-random construction templates in the natural world. Indeed, he would say that such a coincidence in physical appearance indicated the presence of a "guiding purpose" on the part of Mother Nature - unless, and this was always possible, the humans from Earth and the humans from Ixnor had common ancestral ties. No technical apparatus, vehicles or decoration of any kind were to be seen. The bluish glow of the polished rock beneath his feet hinted not only at the use of very advanced technology but also the presence, in large quantities, of extremely pure rock crystals.

Livingstone felt the urge to laugh out loud when he looked at the Commander and Dawson, his second-in-command, both in ceremonial dress (fortunately made of polymer-free materials), flanked by half a dozen uniformed soldiers, in total contrast to the slender feminine figure of the girl and the two men that now calmly approached them, their white semi-transparent tunics rippling in the light breeze, apparently naked beneath them and bare-footed. He stared at Gael, fascinated by the delicately fragile features and feminine sweetness of this beautiful girl, fascinated too by the powerful inner vibrations she seemed to give off, almost as if within or beneath that diaphanous appearance there existed a wise and venerable elder. The two young men that walked by her side had the air of habitual companions at these encounters, moving nimbly and elegantly forward and emitting, or so he thought, an equally harmonic vibration. He immediately took to them both. The contrast between the Earthmen - even he had taken the care to dress formally, as dictated by military regulations - and the Ixnorians was remarkable, however. Though no words had yet been exchanged, the former seemed more artificial than the latter. He looked at Burns and saw, from the lines etched in his forehead and the way his jaws were clenched together, that he felt uncomfortable and irritated. His skin seemed redder than it had a few moments earlier and his decisive air (which he had displayed throughout the landing) had given way to anger and probably uncertainty.

The Commander could hardly believe it. The welcoming committee they had sent him consisted of three half-naked, grinning teenagers. There were no awaiting dignitaries, no vehicles, no music or noise of any sort other than the gentle whistle of the wind in the trees. It was as if he had stumbled across a lost hamlet back home and two or three curious locals that didn't know him from Adam had come to meet him. At first sight, it seemed a sign of contempt, almost an insult. As for Jim Dawson, his air of astonishment also spoke volumes. Had they traversed the Universe only to be met by barefoot children? Was such a hostile, contemptible attitude towards visitors on the part of the leaders of this planet customary? What kind of a madhouse was this? After making contact with a huge ship and taking absolutely no precautions during the initial contacts, they seemed set on demonstrating complete indifference. Unless their customs and traditions were very different... Whatever the case, it was a question of waiting and seeing what happened. At the very least, anything the three may have to say ought to be heard. Even if he did feel a little disappointed, a little irritated and a little uncomfortable.

The three Ixnorians stopped a short distance from the party. Smiling, they placed their hands over their heart and then slowly spread them into a fan shape. As Commander Burns and the other Earthmen responded with an absurd salute, Livingstone - in a state of near ecstasy - savoured the beauty of the movement and the irradiation of pure love which seemed to inwardly accentuate the golden glow of the sun with immense, yet joyous, invigorating power... He attempted to respond with a similar inner and exterior gesture, glad that he had found such an open, constructive and trustworthy attitude. He waited for the dialogue to begin. Surprised, he saw Gael turn towards him, smiling. He then heard the melodious voice of the interplanetary welcoming co-ordinator for the first time.

"Greetings, friend, on behalf of the Planetary Council. I greet all those present and all those that have come to our planet. It is with joy that we welcome you and will do all we can to make your stay a happy and fruitful one."

Embarrassed, Livingstone realised that he had been taken for the leader of the party. This did not overly surprise him, however, as he had been the only one to adequately respond to their greeting; it was also quite probable that the girl could see the auras of those present and his was, perhaps, the most colourful and brilliant. The Commander, a great believer in hierarchy, may not have reacted too well to this, though. And he hadn't. Burns spoke up, dryly, offended at the misunderstanding and, as was to be expected, incapable of understanding its origin.

"I'm sorry but there appears to have been a slight

misunderstanding. I am Commander Hamilton Burns and this is my second-in-command Jim Dawson. I am the captain of Star 1, the ship in orbit around this planet, and would like to extend the greetings of the United States of America, of the Planet Earth and my own." The Commander tried to smile but, to an observer such as Livingstone, it was clearly proving difficult. His voice sounded tense - and, judging from the keen sensitivity of the Ixnorians, would not go unnoticed.

Unflustered but with less of a smile on her face, Gael looked at Commander Burns and then at Livingstone. He felt her large golden brown eyes focus on him. He was sad and embarrassed at the Commander's egocentric and pompous display, and could hardly stand the profoundly innocent yet vibrant beauty of the look she gave him accompanied by the briefest telepathic exchange. Gael felt the answer. She acknowledged his anguished apology and, saving a chance to talk to Livingstone in private until later, prepared to carry on. She felt an affinity with this man and an almost total absence of resonance in relation to the others.

"In that case, my brother, I shall respond in kind. I am Gael, the Interplanetary Welcoming Co-ordinator, and these are my assistants Izar and Nordin. Our planet is open to you so that you might get to know it. You may go where you will and talk with whomsoever you wish."

Gael followed the welcoming procedures despite finding it odd that the expedition was led by a being less luminous than one of his own subalterns and that some of the visitors carried devices that gave off such negative vibrations, devices created to destroy. The first seeds of worry had been sown. It was still to soon to draw conclusions, though, and it would be impolite to scan the visitors without their expressing a desire for her to do so - as frequently happened, since many interstellar travellers wished to reach a state of mutual transparency as soon as possible. This was clearly not the case here...

"I thank you for your trust. We would be very pleased and very interested in learning about your world and your customs. I must confess to being somewhat surprised at the way in which we have been welcomed. I was expecting more people, different circumstances... Is this the way you always welcome visitors from other worlds?"

"Could you explain what you mean?"

"Well, it's rather odd that there are no dignitaries here to meet us, no vehicles, no signs of any sort of protocol."

Burns felt irritated and impatient but also alienated, out of his element. He certainly hadn't expected to be met by this smirking creature. What about protocol? The lengthy ceremonial welcoming? The exchange of technical information? The establishment of plan for exchange?

"I take it that your customs in this area are rather different from our own. I do indeed belong to the Planetary Council of Ixnor and have been appointed to receive you. Our real welcome is an inner one, however. We are deeply interested in sharing what is within and therefore do not waste our energies on external ceremonies..."

Gael quickly realised, even without scanning them, that the Earthmen were - for the most part - sensorially deficient. They had not responded to the irradiation they had been subjected to and seemed to lack any telepathic sense. She found it odd that they had managed to translocate to Ixnor; looking at the navigator, though, who seemed at a loss as to what to do, it began to dawn on her. She felt the loyalty and constructive spirit within him, and at the same time sensed his anguish and embarrassment, looking at his companions as if they were mischievous children about to do a naughty deed. The truth of this situation was clearly distorted by appearances. It would be set straight, but not immediately.

Burns tried to make sense of what he had heard. Perhaps he was being too hasty. After all, customs could be very different. He still found it hard to block out his irritation but he would do what he could, for now...

"I believe I understand. Might I know what we should do next?"
"That depends on your needs, my brother. How can we be of use to you?"

Her familiarity was so odd!

"I should like to have some of my men meet with your specialists and exchange information. I should also like to get to know your planet better and find out about mineral deposits, natural resources..."
"I shall see that you are put in touch with the right people. In the meantime, perhaps you would like to visit one of our cities."

Commander Burns looked at Dawson, then at Livingstone. He didn't quite know what to think. He could see no city or vehicle in the vicinity. He was just about to open his mouth to speak when he saw a small open craft silently floating towards them. It was driven by a middle-aged woman, with abundant hair and penetrating green eyes, rather attractive for someone who was no longer a little girl. She spoke gaily,

"I just received your summons, Gael. Greetings to all of you, dear visitors. I shall be pleased to take you wherever you wish to go. Consider me at your service."

Gael thanked her with her usual smile and a slight tilt of her head.

Then, with an easy, carefree gesture, she had the visitors climb aboard the vessel. It was obvious to the navigator that she was reacting like a kind Earth hostess showing important visitors around her house, the only difference being that she was about to show them around her planet, of which she was one of the highest authorities.

A few moments later, inside the craft, the Interplanetary Welcoming Co-ordinator appeared momentarily distracted as she explained the route they were to take through areas of lush vegetation. Burns whispered to Livingstone,

"Listen here: I didn't hear any summons and I'm sure the girl didn't use any sort of communicator. What is this? Some sort of act? Had they set it up before?"

"My dear Commander", said Livingstone, feeling impatient. "That "girl" as you call her is one of the highest dignitaries on this planet. She summoned her telepathically. In case you haven't yet noticed, we are among a people in relation to which we are little more than opaque, inept beings. They communicate telepathically with the same ease with which we talk, the difference being that their means of communication is more direct, more sincere and bereft of hidden meanings. They do not string together a sequence of words to try to get their message across; they convey it directly, from one mind to the other. They use language to communicate thoughts but most importantly, I believe, to exteriorise their psychic energy. For them, words and telepathy are part of a global process of communication and action."

"How do you know all this? Did they tell you?"

"I feel it."

"You mean that, at this very moment, they can pick up or feel whatever we are thinking?"

"Of course, if they want to. And it makes me glad. I have nothing to hide and I like them very much. They seem sincere, loyal and extremely well intentioned."

Burns fell silent. He had to admit that, to a certain extent, Livingstone was in a far better position than he to understand what was going on. Yet it was worrying that the Ixnorians could read his thoughts without him being able to do anything about it and that Livingstone could communicate with them without him being able to control what was said...

"Listen, Livingstone. You can communicate telepathically with them?"

"Well... Up to a point, yes."

"Can you tell if they're reading our thoughts?"

"Yes. But they're not. They feel it would be rude. They'll communicate verbally unless we make it clear we prefer telepathy. Local ethics appear to dictate that an individual's psychic intimacy must be respected, particularly when the individual is a visitor to the planet."

"If you pick up any intrusion I want to be told at once, do you hear?"

"Certainly."

Livingstone hated lying. Understand he did, but that did not mean he meant to obey. He was beginning to realise that his fellow Earthmen were on the wrong planet. The anxiety he felt was now spinning out of control. It occurred to him that he had brought a group of heavily armed barbarians to a fragile, civilised land.

Gael threw a glance at Livingstone. She did not want to scan his thoughts without his permission, but she could sense his anguish. She sought to console him, reaching out to calm his centres of energy most affected by the painful emotion. The navigator felt the current of vibrant energy, the calm, invigorating support she was providing him, and smiled in gratitude. How wise, how alluring the girl was! There was no doubt she would be capable of curing most diseases on Earth by means of her psychic powers, her irradiation was that strong, that specific, that tender. He felt as if he had known her for a thousand years such was the sense of affinity he felt with her. He was about to let her know she could continue but stopped himself, afraid he might in some way be betraying a loyalty he vaguely owed the planet Earth and his companions.

Burns saw him smile at the beautiful girl and, with a wink, whispered to him,

"Is it just me or have you and the co-ordinator taken to each other? Could be very useful to us, you know."

Livingstone did not answer. He was sickened by the observation, not so much by the words themselves as the thoughts that lay behind them. In his need to control the situation, the Commander was moving into areas that filled him with loathing. Usefulness... Nurturing affection in someone with the sole purpose of using this later; using love as a means of manipulation. Dammit! Why the hell hadn't he found out a bit more about the ethics of these dubious people before he had agreed to translocate them? Had his human brothers journeyed to the end of the Universe only to find a mirror that reflected their aberrations still clearer?

"We are arriving at the Third City of Water", Gael said.

The ship rose above the forest through which they had gently been flying, banked and descended towards a naturally contoured area. And the navigator suddenly felt like a child, being shown a palace made of chocolate.

Chapter 8

The Third City of Water

Despite the colossal size of some of the buildings, they only became completely visible as the ship closed in, harmonious works of art that blended in perfectly with the landscape, they were constructed of natural materials, principally rock. Many of them seemed like simple extensions of natural contours, and looked as if they had been hewn out of the very rock they stood on. Closer inspection revealed that what had seemed little more than hills or large rocks when seen from a distance were in fact elegantly sculptured buildings. Their shapes were somewhat capricious - another similarity with the natural world - but nevertheless hinted at an elaborate architectural culture. As the ship silently descended towards its landing site, the Earthmen noticed with astonishment that the city was filled with the sounds of the wind and, above all, water.

Despite the large numbers of transport vehicles that floated noiselessly through the city, the sound of running water and innumerable waterfalls slowly became more noticeable. The sound was structured, producing a musical effect. The successive points of circulation and different levels of water had been designed in such a way as to create rhythmic and melodious tones, although here and there variations in intensity and differing melodies, could be heard, composed of waterfalls, the burbling of a stream or water falling into differently shaped recipients. Small echo chambers, amplifiers and sound reflectors were located both inside and outside the buildings, and numerous spouts of water of different lengths and widths gushed into small receptacles of equally different shapes and materials. Marvelling at it all, Livingstone listened and felt Gael's explanations as she led them on a brief guided tour through the streets. The Third City of Water owed its name, just like other similar cities, from the painstaking work carried out there into this element and its melodious sound effects. According to the interplanetary welcoming co-ordinator, many Ixnorians in need of rebalancing their nervous system spent several days in these places enjoying the benefits of the "harmonies of the water". Indeed, the whole city had been built to produce aerodynamic effects, which in turn provided a revitalising blend of wind and water sounds. Here and there, the joyous trilling of birds perched in leafy trees complemented the sounds of the sea, river, watercourse, musical waterfall or rain, wisely created by the carefully channelled waters.

There were other cities built around the natural elements too. Gael spoke enthusiastically of the city where she had been born, the First City of the Wind, and its Aeolian harmonies, of the wind channels that existed there, of the ingenious way in which decorative architectural elements had been arranged so as to allow the pitch and resonance of the wind to be altered. There were also the Cities of Stone, rich in crystal, to which many journeyed to cultivate "inner strength and a sense of the Eternal"; the Green Cities, where the focus lay on the "contributions of the vegetable kingdom" and in which many people temporarily set up residence to better "manage their health"; and the "Balanced Cities", where natural elements were combined and arranged with artistic skill. It was in the latter that the majority of the population lived for longer periods. Livingstone felt such a mixture of profound emotions, empathy, joy, gratitude and tenderness towards this people, that he could not find the words to express it. He knew that Gael sensed what he felt, though...

The skills of those driving the silent vehicles all around them were remarkable. There seemed to be such understanding between them, no competition or conflict, even though some of them were travelling at relatively high speed. They gave way to each other, cheerfully waved hello and, when someone seemed in a greater hurry, he or she was at once given right of way. Livingstone understood that as far as the Ixnorians were concerned, there must be strong reasons for somebody to be in a hurry and they therefore deserved consideration. Otherwise they would not be in a hurry. Besides, the Ixnorian sense of sharing meant that everyone co-operated in using the City of Water and its byways.

Burns, Dawson and the other members of the Earth committee looked around, somewhat apprehensively, as they were led towards a building that seemed to have been hewn out of a huge rock. Everything was unusual and unknown to them. The fact that they were currently surrounded by large numbers of smiling Ixnorians, in an atmosphere that would have been all but silent were it not for the occasional voice, the birds, the hum of the wind and the murmur of water, was unexpected and worrying to them. Besides, they had been counting on an armed escort and here they were being led by three barefoot youngsters. Burns could control himself no longer.

"Gael?"
"Yes, my brother?"

The form of address itself was odd: shouldn't they at least use "Madam Welcoming Co-ordinator" and "Commander Burns"?

"Could you tell me the reason why we do not have an escort? Isn't it dangerous to walk around without protection?"

"I'm not sure I fully understand. What should we protect ourselves from?"

"But you're an important person on this planet and we are visitors from far away; couldn't we be mugged, for example?"

Gael had begun to worry, as she feared they may have detected a threat that had escaped her; now, however, it was clear that the Earthmen were simply projecting their fears to the exterior instead of sensing any real danger. Unfortunately, it was just as obvious that this primitive projection mechanism, indicative of a lack of self-awareness and emotional refinement, was typical of the way most of them functioned (she sensed the navigator's wonder and admiration; the "harmonies of the water" appeared to be doing him good).

"Are you referring to the possibility of our being physically attacked or having our possessions stolen?"

"Exactly. I've brought soldiers along with me but we don't know this area. Do we need reinforcements?"

Gael began to feel slightly apprehensive, even more so as at that exact moment she felt embarrassment, shame and a renewed apology on the part of Livingstone. Yet she remained receptive, open and trusting.

"There have been no criminals on this planet for centuries. A long time ago we allowed those that persisted in committing crimes to be transported to other planets, ones where the general level of the population was more in keeping with such tendencies. We do get the odd pathological case, but these are carefully treated and get better quickly."

Burns could not believe it.

"You mean there's no theft? No burglaries? No murders?"

"Basically, no. There's no point. No-one pays particular attention to their own or others' possessions. When we wish to use something, we ask. None of us minds sharing, on the contrary... Besides, we don't give much importance to our personal lives, though we hold life itself as sacred. Who would dare take it?"

"But isn't it possible that someone, for some reason, may wish to do us harm?"

"We would feel the threat."

"Very well, but how would you defend yourselves?"

"By suppressing or dematerialising the source of the threat."

"How is that possible? Wouldn't it require sophisticated weaponry?"

Gael had to give in to the fact that Burns, the non-telepath that he was, would not easily understand. Besides, he had brought soldiers with him and his words betrayed a preoccupation with instruments of war - one of the signs of a pre-cosmic civilisation.

"I believe we will have a chance to explain how we keep the peace. This is not the right time, however. Let me assure you, though: there is no crime."

Burns looked at Dawson, irritated and apprehensive. It was obvious that the girl (he still could not think of her as a high dignitary) was holding something back. Did they have such effective control mechanisms that they could, for example, vaporise any criminal from a distance? And suppose one of them innocently reached out to pick a fruit from one of the many trees around? Might the offending hand not be suddenly disintegrated by some sort of ray fired from who knows where? And who knew what terrible secrets lay behind those smiles and carefree demeanour?

Gael turned cheerfully to Livingstone.

"My brother, I feel that you in particular will appreciate the lodgings we have prepared for you. Everything has been prepared to provide tranquillity and renovation. And I see that our city pleases you. For that I am extremely happy."

As she spoke these simple words, her face and eyes seemed to light up. What a marvellous creature! As he openly thought this it was instantly picked up by Gael, who then appeared to reach out and touch his own heart in thanks. Livingstone also thanked her in words, happy at the warm, benevolent atmosphere of the place, now feeling slightly more relaxed thanks to the beauty that surrounded him. Perhaps his fears were exaggerated. His companions must have some notion of the responsibility involved in making contact with a different civilisation and would surely not cause any trouble. In the meantime, they had arrived at their destination. The building was relatively small (only ten storeys high) and constructed along an escarpment. Its façade was covered with a stone-like crust, making it almost indistinguishable from the rock against which it leant, although its cylindrical shape meant it wasn't quite flush with the stone. The building did resemble just another rock, though. One with windows, doors and a few set-back openings that appeared to be verandas of some sort. Some of these were filled with bushes which may have grown there naturally, with no human interference, were it not for their carefully trimmed shape.

As they entered and walked down a long dome-shaped corridor, they were surprised at just how well lit the interior was. The answer lay in an enormous skylight through which shone luminous rays, crossing the hollow interior of the building and striking a strange group of crystals. At the same time, they began to pick up a delicately soft tinkling, the unmistakable sound of water falling drop by drop in small streams; this time, however, the musical effect was of an indescribable beauty, at once soft and clear, "the sonic equivalent of a stained glass window", the navigator thought. Indeed, the sculpture at the centre of the building was made of crystal, rivulets and streams of water cascading down its sides and driving moveable parts, which resonated as they touched. The tinkling of the crystal, the burbling of the water and the kaleidoscopic effect of the light were too much for Livingstone. A tear slipped down his cheek as he smiled, conveying his joy at being there. To the surprise of the Earthmen, Gael approached Livingstone and carefully collected the teardrop on the tip of her finger. She then moved to the crystal sculpture and dipped her finger in the water. She turned back, smiling.

"Thank you for contributing to the vibration of this place."

Livingstone suddenly felt the urge to embrace her.

"Thank *you*, my sister, for bringing us here."

Burns could not just stand by.

"On behalf of us all, I should also like to express our thanks. This is indeed a charming place and I believe I speak for us all when I say how fine we feel here."

"I am glad to hear it. I will now show you to your lodgings. Whenever you wish, you are free to wander the city and meet its inhabitants. I shall then leave you alone for a few hours to get settled."

Later, alone in the apartment that had been selected for him, Livingstone gazed through the enormous inside window overlooking the crystal sculpture, taking stock of his situation. This was better than a fairy story. He regretted that his companions were unable to comprehend how psychically advanced the Ixnorians were and the care with which they were being treated, but this did not prevent him from appreciating the stunning combination of light, sound and vibration that he could feel rekindling his strength and enveloping him in well-being. He felt more at home here than on his home planet.

Not far away, Burns, Dawson and Ryan, another Star 1 officer, were discussing recent events.

"To tell the truth", Ryan said, "I feel great here. It's not Earth, granted, but you have to admit it's not bad..."

"Agreed", replied the Commander. "We've had no reasons to complain so far and have been treated kindly. Even so, I find everything so hard to interpret. We need to stay on our toes."

Dawson spoke up.

"I'm sorry, sir, but I think it's important that we keep an open mind. Their traditions and customs are obviously very different from our own. I can't really see what reasons you might have to distrust them?"

"None, for now. But it is possible they have some interest in our ship. Don't you find it odd that they haven't even mentioned it? And how the hell can they guarantee that a murderer wouldn't constitute a threat? And what guarantees do *we* have that, right now, we're not being watched by some advanced surveillance system we have no knowledge of?"

"They might have bad intentions, but then again they might not. They seem so carefree that I think they probably are. We, on the other hand, have certain reasons to be pleased at what our sensors have indicated, do we not, Commander?"

The smile on Dawson's face was almost crafty. Luckily, Burns thought, that navigator wasn't around to appreciate it. It might have led to a certain cooling off of their relations...

"Indeed. The planet's mineral resources cannot be overlooked. I'm certain we can negotiate the transport of a large quantity of precious minerals. As long as they don't want too much in return."

"Such as?"

"I don't know. I'm afraid something may lurk behind their apparent simplicity."

"And what about Livingstone? He seems to like it here. And the girl seems to have taken a liking to him", said Ryan.

"Best to keep him in the dark. I'm not sure what's going through his mind right now, but I don't trust him. If we tell him our priorities don't just include the search for knowledge, who's to say he won't give us away?"

Livingstone was looking out of the window, fascinated by the atmosphere of the building, when he felt something akin to a surge of refreshing energy. He looked behind him, searching for its source. It was Gael - and she was sparkling more than ever.

The Interplanetary Welcoming Co-Ordinator

The Welcoming Co-ordinator gently approached him, looking deep into his eyes. He could write volumes on the feelings she awoke in him, the navigator thought. The girl motioned him to sit down on a cushion next to her. The interrogation was evident and he felt it. But, as if to make him feel more at home, Gael spoke.

"My brother, I believe the time has come to set a few things straight. We need to make things clear. You are different from your companions and, undoubtedly, the most up to the task. I feel there is an enormous difference between your personal exteriorisation and their own, and it intrigues me. I also feel a profound affinity with you and wish to get to know you better."

"Thank you, my sister. I too feel this affinity in a clear and intense way. Unfortunately, as you know, I'm concerned because I have brought the ship here."

"I sense a part of what you might have to say. Even so, please go on."

"Most of the people on my planet have not yet learnt to harvest their inner potential. We still have large numbers of criminals; we have wars in which technologically advanced weapons are used to take human lives by the thousands or millions. There are forms of commercial warfare too, in which lives aren't taken directly, but which can ruin the economies of entire countries, or at the very least, ruin companies and bring misery to large numbers of workers."

Livingstone's words reflected his bitterness and shame. He felt he stood before the wisest, purest, most beautiful creature he had ever met. It filled him with pleasure but, at the same time, depressed him. He was talking about a family of which he was ashamed, as if his fellow Earthmen were its black sheep. And yet he didn't feel he was betraying anything or anyone, simply stating the truth. Besides, he had the feeling that, should the leaders of Ixnor decide to find out all there was to know about the Earthmen, there was nothing anyone could do to stop them.

"I have difficulty in understanding what you are telling me. You speak of your own people as if they were a pre-cosmic civilisation unfit for the responsibility of interstellar contact. The Law of the Cosmos seems to imply that beings at such a stage of development and awareness are incapable of making such contacts. And yet you are capable of translocation and that requires advanced psychic abilities."

"The truth is that it was merely by chance that we gained the knowledge of translocation. We discovered it when a ship crash-landed on our planet after being hit by a piece of orbiting space refuse. That's how we learnt the secret."

Gael stared at him incredulously.

"You mean that you still haven't travelled or made contact outside your own planet? And you brought such a huge ship?"

“That’s right. This is the first time we’ve ventured out into interstellar space.”

“But why such a big ship? Why so many people on board?”

“I was told it provided hope for mankind, that it could help to establish colonies, bring back new found knowledge, the raw materials we needed. They said it would expand our awareness. But I’m starting to get the feeling they didn’t tell me everything. It’s quite possible they lied to me.”

“Let me see if I understand... They still lie on your planet?”

Gael felt the truth of what he was saying. But it was unthinkable that a civilisation able to distort the truth could have traversed such enormous distances. If that was what had happened, though, the reason for the man’s anguish would begin to show itself in his spirit. A man who seemed too aware of himself to get caught up in such an intense, almost unbalancing emotion. Unless the cause was sufficiently serious and went beyond his personal interests... Livingstone’s reply was a mental echo.

“Unfortunately, my sister, most of us find it easy to cheat and lie if there is personal gain to be made. I say this with sadness.”

The co-ordinator stood up and moved away a little, a heavy expression on her face. She then slowly looked him up and down. Livingstone knew she was scrutinising his aura and waited patiently. She smiled again.

“You don’t lie, do you?”

“Never.”

“You don’t steal or use violence?”

“No. I think I would be capable of using violence but only to defend myself.”

“Are there many like you on your planet? Is it possible that the others predominate? You know, I find it hard to accept that the ship in which you came is commanded by beings that are less luminous than you... That's why I took you for the captain."

"Unfortunately, people that feel and think like me are rare. Most Earthmen are still individualistic, competitive, egocentric. They believe in looking after number one. I'm still not sure whether we aren't on the road to self-destruction. For many years polluting technologies have plundered our natural environment and the level of our seas is rising, threatening our coastal towns, the most important ones, generally speaking. One of the prices we have paid for destroying nature is global warming. That may be one of the reasons why Earth leaders sent such a large ship into space."

The co-ordinator withdrew into herself, her eyes half closed. A few moments later she sat down next to Livingstone again, still smiling.

"You've been worried. I partly understand the reason for your concern, but tell me: as an individual, do you fear you have committed some sort of error?"

"I do. I'm afraid that by agreeing to translocate the ship, I have endangered a civilisation that is far more advanced but far less aggressive than our own. I don't feel I have reasons to fear you, but perhaps you have reasons to fear us."

Gael did not hesitate. She appeared not even to give his words a second thought.

"I regret that an unaware, pre-cosmic civilisation has been able to venture into the cosmos. Yet I know that there is an inherent wisdom in the whole of the Universe. We do not understand it but we know that it builds or allows events to happen according to designs that often escape us. And the truth is you're here. Perhaps you represent the best side of your planet. And I feel a deep affinity with you, as if I'd known you for a thousand years. Do you recognise this affinity?"

Livingstone felt a strange mixture of emotions, shame and anguish, intense joy and tenderness. Gael made him feel young again. Insecure but intensely alive, able to do creative, crazy things.

"I recognise the affinity. I should like to get to know you better, my sister. I am beginning to regret having brought my companions here, but I do not regret being with you. I feel more at home than on my own planet. Let me tell you, though, that there's one thing I don't believe you've understood: the ship in which I came could represent a threat to you. A terrible threat!"

Gael stared at him.

At that moment, the navigator saw an unexpected light in the eyes of the co-ordinator. He knew the meaning of this sudden flash - it reflected her almost unfathomable psychic power. Beneath her apparently diaphanous appearance lay tremendous power. He was certain of it. Inside, this young, delicate creature was capable of unleashing cyclonic forces. He then heard her speak quietly, her voice soft, almost maternal, as if trying with all her heart to reassure a troubled soul.

"If the threat grows, we will know about it in good time. Your fellow travellers would never be able to destroy the cosmic order. You need have no fears about this. Please believe me."

Livingstone was baffled. It was hard to know whether she knew what nuclear weapons or laser cannons really were. On the other hand, it could be that as far as she was concerned they were just deadly toys in the hands of aggressive children. He tried to believe.

"The idea that we may somehow endanger your civilisation or your planet fills me with disgust. So I shall try to believe you."

The co-ordinator smiled at him as she moved closer. Then, taking him gently by the right hand - knowing telepathically that the gesture was welcome – said:

"I ask you to temporarily forget your concerns. I also ask: would you like to know me?"

Livingstone sensed the depth of the question and the psychic possibilities involved. Gael was referring to nothing less than baring her body and her soul. He found it hard to believe that a creature such as her could offer so much as, by Earth standards, they hardly knew each other. Here, standards were different though. Deep down they seemed strangely familiar.

"I would like to know you, my sister. I should also like to be known. Teach me, please."

Gael motioned for him to kneel before her. Then, also kneeling, she took him gently by the right hand and placed it over her chest while she placed her own hand on his. She closed her eyes, preparing for the state of total communion.

"Look deep within and reveal your soul to me. Totally."

He knew that she was going to do the same and immediately assented, closing his eyes. He breathed deeply, relaxing as he received Gael's energy, allowing her fragrance, her breathing, her very existence to penetrate him. At the same time, his own energy began to flow as he focused on his body's centres of energy and joined them with hers. He then gave himself up totally, letting their deepest souls do the talking...

A spiral of energy between them, enveloping them. Multicoloured lights dancing between their bodies, between their centres of energy, between their souls. A sweet, continual sound, a mixture of wind and rain and songs and moans and sighs and laughter and anything else natural. Expanded awareness. A shift in being. A shift in sensation, feeling, thought. The cosmos was man and woman. Gael as a child, Gael laughing and crying and singing. Livingstone child and Livingstone man. Livingstone in pain and Livingstone content. Gael and Livingstone on parallel paths, a thousand coincidences millions of light years apart for most of their lives. Their hearts beating together as one. Breathing as one. Minds joined, sharing, the harmony ever more complete as they merged. Livingstone couldn't tell where he ended and she began, where she ended and he began; nor did he want to. He didn't know where his awareness of the Cosmos began and where hers began and vice-versa. It was a unique, indescribable experience, far beyond human understanding, infinitely different from the human idea of intercourse.

Gael was inside him, with all her joy and all her knowledge, delicately feminine in all her immense psychic power, her aura flashing with light, and he was inside her, a wise, mature, solitary man who still knew how to feel and live like a child, playing in a world still so full of pain... Hopes and disappointments, breakthroughs, strength and rest and a thousand tiny, subtle, everyday details; meditating on mountains, in valleys, on beaches, in houses, alone or accompanied, on a thousand different themes. The experience of an Earthman and an Ixnorian. Two worlds overlapping. Two books of life overlapping. Two cultures unveiling themselves mutually. Their bodies and souls in unison, merged together as one.

When they were finally finished, Livingstone had lost all notion of time. He deeply loved and profoundly knew Gael, who deeply loved and profoundly knew him in turn. His life would never be the same again. To say that he had found the woman he had been yearning for all his life would be an understatement. If he wanted to put it in words, it would be better to simply say that he and her were one. Simply... (and the tears rolling down his face were tears of joy - and so were hers).

Chapter 10

Childhood

The navigator remained under the effect of their inner exchange. His mind and brain were still processing information and trying to make sense of it. And, as was typical in him, one of the threads that ran through this processing and understanding was the notion of a path, of personal history. Provided it was clear to what extent it was still alive in each person's present.

He and Gael had led very different lives. Now, however, their paths had converged. Livingstone clearly saw how difficult it had been to rid himself of the educational constraints of his past and become a freer, more flexible, fuller human being. His long education had centred, amongst other things, on the "art" of differentiating between and defining concepts. The separation of body and intellect, reflected in the experiencing of physical education and all other subjects or in the imposed need to restrict body movement during lessons. The separation of intellect and emotion, the fact that the student-teacher relationship was predominantly intellectual and should not allow emotions to interfere with it. It was hard for a teacher to have individual emotional relationships with dozens and dozens of students (and if this did happen with one or two in particular, it would be seen as favouritism). During his time at secondary school and university, such a relationship was viewed with suspicion - frowned on by teachers and students alike: the former could be accused of corrupting minors or taking advantage of their position of power to obtain sexual favours; the latter could be accused of trying to get good grades by illicit means. And both situations actually occurred with some frequency. As such, social preconceptions coupled with such large numbers of students led to an apparent divorce between emotion and intellect - which in no way made the underlying emotion vanish, but simply moved it to the psychic subconscious. This in turn could lead the (apparently) most intellectual of scientists to displays of immature emotional behaviour (anger, depression, abruptness, preconception) when, for example, their convictions were questioned. How different might things be if his schooling had condemned him to only partially develop his emotional side (and his intuition too, thought Livingstone)? And then there was the idea of objectivity and exteriority, since it was considered imperative to avoid letting emotional or intellectual values interfere with one's ability to observe the world. As a result, anything that hinted at interiority and subjectivity had to be eradicated (even if, in the meantime, quantum physics was demonstrating that the human mind was able to influence "objective" phenomena and that the act of observation could materially define the object observed).

The need to "sterilise" knowledge of all "emotional contamination" was taken to extremes. It placed great importance on the use of highly detailed, sequential language exempt of alternative meanings, the antithesis of poetry, to ensure the scientific nature of communication. Yet, in certain minds, this produced ideas regarding the real nature of the world that were too linear - as they only learnt to see through the prism of "Science", forgetting that there were others ways of looking. And this in turn made science all the poorer, concealing important portions of reality. What kind of a reality was it that had to be limited to what could be put into words or graphically represented - through speech or scientific symbols - and to what could be repeatedly observed and tested by scientific methods? Then there was the power struggle within the world of science, even within some faculty of science student residences. These conflicts were often little more than attempts at personal gain disguised as theoretical differences; yet how could university intellectuals see this? They were trained to ignore emotions which, hidden away, led to the adoption of unethical, immature and ignoble attitudes. Other intellectuals allowed their emotions and creativity to surface outside their academic circles but, once back at their university, institute or other place devoted to the production of knowledge and technology, did their best to ignore them.

Livingstone had had his fair share of good and bad teachers. Some were great followers of the parrot-fashion method of learning, others sought to bring knowledge into the lives of their students by recreating it in each class. Some had left knowledge strictly imprisoned between the walls of the kind of cold reasoning "allowed" by the legitimate methods of each subject. Livingstone himself had suffered from "intellectualitis", like many of his colleagues, and had spent years of his life convinced that emotion, creativity or irrationality were nothing more than sentimental stumbling blocks on the path to knowledge. Even if the great moments of genius in the past on the part of those scientists, philosophers, artists and religious men that had built civilisation, often seemed to precede rationalisation and discursive demonstration... He was already suffering from what, for some, were excessive ethical concerns, however: for this reason he had run into trouble with various colleagues and been forced to make an exceptional effort to defend himself in these academic skirmishes without becoming competitive. On countless occasions his "friends" had refused to provide him with information he was unable to obtain on his own or with material covered in lessons he had missed for the sole purpose of attempting to gain some sort of advantage. And he had always given his colleagues all the help he could, had never kept an interesting book or new article to himself.

He had received his best education outside university when he began his own search. He remembered his time at kindergarten when it was important to cultivate affection and fantasy, and the way in which, as the years went by, this was considered "immature", "inexact" or some other such cliché used by the academics. The fidgety, loving child, the simple child, the lovesick teenager in love, and other characters he had played had been locked away in cellars once the doors to secondary school and university had been opened. Funny: the opening of what were supposed to be "higher doors" to reasoning and logic was looked on as being incompatible with other areas that were essential to human development; when these doors had opened it had proved necessary to close many others and amputate parts of the human being. He had thus become partially incomplete and cut off from himself by the need to adapt to the academic environment. His scholarly activities had progressively focused on intellectual virtues and, as if on a Procrustean bed, anything that was beyond or behind intellectual reasoning was doomed to the dubious lands of superstition, anti-scientific emotionality, poetry that was incompatible with methodical reasoning. The sap of life had all but dried up in many places of "learning" since these spent more time examining "anatomisable" corpses than living beings or objects within their context. His post-graduate training thus concentrated largely on undoing what he had learnt at university. Gradually, his inner need led him to regain fantasy and affection, intuition, poetry and many other ways of understanding and creating. Schools had been very useful to him, but his best education had come before and after them. And yet life had also prepared him to meet Gael. And she had had quite a different education.

Gael was born in the First City of Wind to benefit, as she re-entered the world, from its aeolic harmonies (because of the mission her parents foresaw for her) but was brought up in a "Balanced City", where the various elements of the natural world helped the physical and psychic development of the child. Her parents had planned her conception with sacramental precision and consciously created the energy field inside which the interchange of bodies had sparked fertilisation and the subsequent growth of organic tissue. This had taken place on the Norya Plateau - as they sensed that the coming child would have something to do with the Ixnor's relations with other worlds. They had consciously lured the child which had approached their auras, in order to facilitate the first connection with the body it would use in its new journey through the densest level of the world. They had then fondly accompanied the whole of the gestation period so as to contribute towards the development of a healthy and harmonic body, their souls and psycho-biophysical systems communicating with the reincarnating soul and the system that grew in the mother's uterus. Later, in the outside world, the bond continued until, aged seven, the child began to extensively exercise free will. The relationship remained a close one, but now the child's own decisions were respected. Up until then, there had been many long and delicate moments of exchange with the bodies, the emotions and thoughts of her parents in an atmosphere filled with melodious sounds.

From the beginning to the end of the more standardised side of her path, schools were places of integral training freely sought by Gael the child, then Gael the adolescent and Gael the adult, who kept consciously within her the capacity for being a child, adolescent and teenager. From a young age, in fact, children's games led them to play the role of adults or adolescents in the same way that adults' games often led them to play the role of children.

Gael's classes had been richer in words at the beginning than at the end of her education since that was the natural progression of things: the child learnt to speak, learned to communicate through words but, as time went by, learned to use their energy as they consciously passed beyond verbal reasoning and absorbed new forms of knowledge for which words were unsuitable. By going beyond her mind, Gael had gone beyond words and entered into internal, direct contact with the "world of meaning" - that which Livingstone called intuition. Lessons were always preceded by moments of meditation: silent and static in some cases, soothing the body, emotions and thoughts, and animated in others, paying special attention and searching for a special presence in the movement of the body, feelings and thoughts. That was where dance, expression through action, expressive vocalisation and work on posture and the "places of the body" came in.

Telepathy had always been present - more in adults than in children once words were no longer considered a special means of expression and understanding - helping to clarify and internally monitor multiple pedagogical experiences. Lessons had thus shifted from a verbal and less telepathic stage to one that was more telepathic, followed at the Ixnorian equivalent of university by an intuitive stage during which students increasingly learned to capture and create the knowledge necessary for contact with the inner nature of things. And, during this time, work on the "inner universe" was accompanied by work on "opening up to the Cosmos". The mind was valued for its creative ability but also the extent to which it could order experience, and was worked as an instrument in each individual's journey to new states of consciousness and, with them, new openings to internal and external cosmic wisdom for each human being. The Earth concept of intelligence was given little worth since it represented an unbalanced cultivation in many cases, of the skill of mentally representing things, with the risk of mistaking the way things looked for reality and clinging to it in a pathological state described as "mental separation".

Lessons were given in a "relaxation state atmosphere" which favoured openness, receptivity and creativity. In this state, the children learnt the equivalent of formal Ixnorian knowledge in a profoundly experiential manner. Even the chemistry experiments described in the crystals of knowledge, the Ixnorian equivalent of Earth text books, were accompanied by suggestions for using one's creative imagination: "Imagine that you're part of the water and as it starts to boil you feel light, light... Then you rise into the air and discover you're not water any more". Affection was brought into awareness and developed through experimentation, such as stroking animals, trying to discover what birds felt as they flew or fish as they swam. Touching different soils, embracing each other (which was considered an art as it implied making contact with the other person and exchanging energy with him or her at various levels; it was thus practised throughout a child's education as part of the syllabi). The senses were fine-tuned and developed, both externally and internally, so that even to an Ixnorian child the Earthmen appeared sensorially deficient, as if some of their senses were missing and others dulled. Tuning them, however, was a simple affair - although guided by experienced teachers - and involved smelling flowers and trying to understand them, feeling the wind on one's face, listening to it rustling in the trees, following the "intentions of the wind", in other words the flow of its energy when oriented by the great subtle builders of nature, looking carefully at the mountains and feeling the pleasure of looking or noticing the blood flowing through their veins, the beating of their heart, the air flowing into their lungs, and synchronising this with the breathing and internal rhythm of high places. The children also learnt how to feel which part of their body responded most to the other living beings (animals and plants) with which they came into contact, to feel the existence of the builders of vegetable forms, the energy corresponding to each emotion or thought pattern. The children were trained from an early age in understanding the alphabet of shapes and colours of thought and emotions, trained to observe the energy auras of living beings and fixed objects (yet with internal movement).

One of the highlights of Gael's childhood was the magical time during which Liriel, the watcher of the Planetary Council - also known as the Weaver of Nature, took her to observe, both inside and outside, her work. She watched her mentally working the delicate weave of the threads of energy of the natural world of Ixnor, great coloured, glittering lines, some flowing through the planet, others flowing across its surface, and she felt the connection of these lines with certain "places of quality" where they joined and intersected. Here, beings with enormous auras that were intimately linked with Liriel could be found, the communion of minds serving to ensure the stability of the energy structure of the natural world. And all this took place with joyful, luminous movement, full of vigour, light, and transparency. The enchanted child realised that beneath the apparent solidity of solid things lay a universe of transparent energies constantly materialised by the minds of marvellous beings, which at that time, seemed mysterious and incomprehensible to her... Yet she soon began to realise that the different shapes of Ixnor's mineral crust were the result and exteriorisation of energy qualities managed by conscious beings but not in the sense she had known until then. There was awareness in the rocks, even in their micro-particles, and there were forms of synthetic awareness in the large mountain ranges. Feeling that everything was alive filled her with such joy that she felt she would explode! Even areas where animal, vegetable and mineral life were especially concentrated had a reason to be and their own logic. Everything had a soul, qualified energy, and that was why it felt so good to be in different places to learn and develop different qualities.

It seemed to Livingstone that Gael had been brought up in a fairy tale, an enchanted land where love and harmony reigned; nothing was done to avoid suffering, however, although when it did happen, everything was done to help those afflicted to accept it and deal with it.

The Ixnorians also had hard or difficult things to do sometimes. So he wasn't surprised that development of the will and also relaxation and non-resistance to painful events were also part of school syllabi.

Great care was taken, then, in developing qualities which seemed pertinent to one's capacity to live and expand. Gael's recollections on these matters were grouped around themes and associated experiences. She had learnt to grow by observing and feeling - and encouraging - the growth of flowers and small animals. She had learnt to develop the sense of her body and to choose the tastes and smells of those foods which her body needed more, "feeling" and anticipating the organic balance or imbalance they might produce if they were consumed. She had learnt stability and permanence sitting atop mountains, in contact with the mineral kingdom and with things that were apparently fixed but which vibrated, vibrated... She had learnt about renewal, her teacher the ocean itself, feeling the relation of the waves and the tides with the coming and going of things and "breathing with the sea", that liquid mass which absorbed, accumulated and transformed so much light... She had learnt self-will by training her body to remain still when this became uncomfortable and all it wanted to do was move or continuing to move when her body was tired and wanted to rest. And then there was that moment which was even more intense than the others when she learnt about health. When she learnt to feel the qualitative differences in her energy as it flowed through the organs of her body and learnt how to feel when something was not right. She had thus learnt 'creative visualisation', to "see health" as a mental image of how her energy and organs would look when everything was all right, and 'transforming visualisation', to "create health" by mentally returning her body to a state of harmony. And how good it had been to learn to "irradiate health" using both techniques to provide healing energy for others... And how all this had been connected, some time later, with general learning on creation through the destruction and recreation of natural materials that could be shaped, transformed, painted, solidified or liquefied.

How could you not love Gael when you knew the life she had led? And how could someone know so much in so little time? Livingstone was stunned and intensely happy.

Chapter 11

High-Level Conference

By Earth time only ninety minutes or so had passed since Livingstone had been led to his quarters. Some of the instants of his energy and psychic exchange with Gael had lasted for centuries, however, each second equivalent to many, many years. Eternity was present in their intense spiritual interchange and had revealed some unexpected facts. The spiritual entity travelling inside Livingstone had known the spiritual entity travelling inside Gael for thousands of years. By exteriorising in human shapes localised in time and space they had made contact various times in different worlds and dimensions of existence. Now, reunited, there was nothing to prevent them from opening up to each other, giving, trusting. There was still a lot to be done, but in Livingstone's brain, little by little, a profound knowledge and understanding of Ixnorian culture and Gael, its representative, was taking shape.

As one, the Interplanetary Welcoming Co-ordinator and the navigator of the Earth ship Star 1 headed for Commander Burns' quarters. As had been arranged, he and the other Earthmen were waiting to be called. The Commander was surprised to see them arrive together but, believing he understood what was going on, discreetly winked at Livingstone, who in turn forced a smile back at him - a smile that was little more than facial muscles and teeth he thought, as inside he felt sickened by the Commander's gesture. Gael spoke up.

"Commander Burns, I have the honour of requesting you to accompany me to a high-level meeting with our highest dignitaries, Axor, the planet leader, and Liriel, the watcher of the Planetary Council."

The Earthman smiled, satisfied. Something normal had finally happened. They were going to establish formal diplomatic contact. The care put into their dress and the documentation they had brought from Earth was justified after all...

The same ship, that had brought them from Finder 3 to this curious building that had welcomed them, was waiting at its exit. Alin, the driver, gently nodded her head in greeting and motioned for them to get in. Then, the only sound being that of the wind, the vessel rose into the air as its top closed over a glass dome. It headed at high speed towards the Crystal Star, situated on top of a huge mountain chain at another point on the planet.

On the way they flew over a vast blue sea dotted with a few vessels. These were predominantly oval-shaped, which seemed rather inappropriate for the high seas. Some of them had darker, rounded areas in their centre, which greatly intrigued Dawson. He took out his binoculars for a closer look. The central area seemed made of glass and there were several men and women grouped around it. They seemed to be watching something. Dawson had to satisfy his curiosity.

"Excuse me, Alin, can you tell me what those boats are doing? I presume they're fishing vessels, or do they have some other function?"

"What do mean, brother?"

"Well, I'm talking about fishing boats. Maritime vessels specialising in catching fish from the sea for food or sport."

The driver of the airship stared at him, incredulous yet at the same time with no hint of judgement. She looked at Gael and exchanged a few quick impressions with her on the primitiveness that seemed to lay behind the simple question. She then spoke calmly, although she felt somewhat apprehensive. The man's sensitivity seemed dulled to such an extent that he was unable to really feel the animal kingdom. As if non-human animals were objects and, even as objects, their natural vibration and bond with their own environment were not to be respected.

"I fail to see the sense in taking animals out of their environment, particularly for food or sport. And we do not eat elements of the animal kingdom for a variety of reasons, one of which is the fact that it would disturb the planet's psychic harmony. The actual physical death of these animals would tend to bring about a disturbance by the emotional suffering it caused... And how could we tolerate that and look on it as sport? I find it hard to understand you."

"But what do you eat then? I haven't seen any cattle anywhere."

"We eat vegetables and minerals in the proportions that seem correct to us. Those boats are there for a simple reason: fellowship."

"What do you mean by that?"

"My friends down there on the ocean are making contact with marine animals and fish. They give them support and ask them if they are well. They observe them and sometimes tell them where the best feeding grounds are to be found."

"But how is that possible?"

"It's easy for us to find the areas richest in suitable foods. We then just transmit an image of them. Their elementary minds pick this up and they're guided to the correct spot. They're guided mentally, not by smell.”

Dawson felt he was treading on sensitive ground and fell silent. It appeared that if they wanted to avoid a serious incident, they would have to eat whatever it was the Ixnorians provided for them. And how good a fresh baked fish might have tasted. It seemed strange, almost stupid to him, but it was best not to take any risks. When all was said and done, even the experience of Earth anthropologists showed that eating habits was an area that should be handled with extreme caution when making contact with different peoples. On the other hand, perhaps they really could direct whole schools of fish...

As they approached the nerve centre of Ixnor, they noticed a huge construction whose shapes were truly those of natural rock crystal, several buildings grouped around a central area, laid out in star formation. They glittered and flashed in the sunlight, the translucent material of which their different sections were made appearing to give off its own strong light. It was breathtakingly beautiful to behold. It almost seemed as if extraordinarily pure and well-proportioned quartz crystals had bloomed there - were it not for the fact that the largest of them, rising vertically up from the centre, was at least seventy storeys high... Amazed, Livingstone gave thanks for merely being allowed to sit there and stare at this architectural colossus, vibrating with such intensity that it almost appeared to be alive, glittering and shining with a shifting, pulsating brilliance, so much so that the wind seemed to draw a series of melodious hums from within... At the same time, the intense psychic vibration emitted by this place made him dizzy, almost to the point where he could no longer stand it, yet it also made him feel exultant, on the edge of ecstasy. He felt his consciousness, twinned with Gael’s, expand and unfold into worlds of peace, joy and resplendent vision. Deep down, he knew that somehow, the wisdom of a thousand planets was stored here. He looked at his fellow Earthmen.

Burns, Dawson, Ryan and the others showed signs of nausea and physical discomfort. Their faces were white, expressions of tension and sickness on them.

"Are you all right, Commander?" the navigator asked.

"This is an amazing place but I feel sick and my head aches. I think that the energy here is harming us somehow, but our scanners don't show any signs of radioactivity or electromagnetism. Don't you feel the same?"

"No, Commander. I can assure you I feel fantastic. What you're feeling is simply the result of the lack of a suitable response on the part of your body to psychic vibrations that are extremely powerful yet too subtle for you to pick up."

"Yeah, right. And why aren't you affected?"

"Because I have practised meditation for thirty-five years. I'm used to it. Even so, I need to adapt."

"Is there any danger to us?"

"No, not if we don't stay here too long. You'll probably have a splitting headache later, but nothing a good night's sleep won't cure. I think they were right in wanting to give us some time before bringing us here. In fact, the only reason they met us so quickly was your insistence on making contact with the planet leaders."

Livingstone's tone was not lost on Burns. The navigator was holding him directly responsible for his own discomfort. He reacted with irritation.

"And what guarantees do I have that we're not being targeted by some deliberate form of psychic attack?"

"For the love of God, man, look around you and try to feel things. These people mean us well and are receiving us out of respect for our free will. You can't blame them for constantly working with powerful psychic vibrations. This is the planet's energy centre. If you want to leave and come back later they won't mind."

"Never! I've faced tough situations before and this doesn't scare me."

Burns turned to the other members of his committee.

"Are we all agreed?"

They were. Nobody wanted to lose face - especially in front of the Commander - and although they felt on the edge of collapse, they could take it. Besides, what they were seeing was fascinating and called out to the best part of them. Leave when they could be so close to such wonders? Who could do such a thing and not regret it later? Who could say, when they returned to Earth, that they had been on the verge of entering the marvellous centre of government of the planet Ixnor and had turned back because of a little sickness?

"Very well, Commander. We go on. Later I shall do my best to lessen the consequences" (they won't understand that - he thought - but I'd better try to diminish the effects).

They landed on a rocky platform close to the Crystal Star. There, surprisingly, they were met by a small group of children of both sexes dressed in pastel coloured tunics, that ran up to Gael and kissed her joyfully. They all seemed between seven and fourteen years old, some of them adolescents already, and gave off a special form of tenderness which wasn't merely childish. Perhaps they were wiser than the overwhelming majority of adult Earthmen, thought Livingstone. Accompanied by the children, the Interplanetary Welcoming Co-ordinator then led them down a long transparent passageway which came out in the Hall of Exchange. This was a circular chamber, a good fifty-five metres in diameter, situated inside one of the enormous crystalline structures. The ceiling was incredibly high and produced a breathtaking effect that far outdid any Earth cathedral. Livingstone clearly sensed that behind the soft yet brilliant ambient light there lay another, immeasurably more powerful and partially latent light. He understood that, if it were revealed, his companions would not survive and he himself may not withstand it. He did not feel afraid, though, but rather a profound and reverent respect - and great joy.

In the centre of the Hall of Exchange was a vast circular area, pinkish in colour, which appeared to consist of carefully polished natural crystals. At its edge, sitting peacefully in a cross-legged position on top of two of the dozens and dozens of small equally circular translucent platforms, were Axor and Liriel. They looked around twenty years old and wore light, unadorned tunics, his a whitish blue colour, hers pinkish white, and had small transparent cloaks with symbols on them: triangles within circles and, within the triangles, cups with stars. Both brought their right hands up on a level with their heart; then, slowly and elegantly, they described an arc, rotating their wrists outwards and extending their arms, their fingers fanned out, towards the newcomers. Fascinated, the navigator saw a powerful burst of energy, a festival of subtle colours, materialise from their hands and reach out towards the group. He was immediately overcome by a feeling of near ecstasy and as his inner vision savoured the vibrating marvel, which was also the auras of the two beings, their energy centres glowing and spinning frenetically, he sought to respond with the gesture he had seen Gael use hours before as a greeting. The other Earthmen imitated his action, repeating the movement but not its meaning nor its energy content. There was no way this would be lost on such beings, which left Livingstone embarrassed, yet again, on behalf of all mankind...

The children sat down around the Planetary Leaders. Livingstone felt like laughing, smiling, weeping, as he felt these timeless yet young-looking entities gazing at him. At his side, Gael's unwavering tenderness helped him to remain calm.

Burns felt disoriented in the middle of the huge hall. The beauty of the place was overpowering. He was still in great pain but, at the same time, was trying to appear normal, even if it was odd that they had been sent a bunch of skipping children as a welcoming committee... Following Gael's indications and the friendly, welcoming gesture of Axor and Liriel, he sat on one of the small circular platforms. The other Earthmen did the same. Then Axor spoke, his rich, deep voice revealing the perfect acoustics of the hall. There was no need for him to strain to make himself heard in any corner of the huge room. It was also remarkable that he spoke their language almost as if it were his own, showing a stunningly fast ability to learn. The first contacts between the Ixnorians and the Earthmen had taken place a mere three days earlier.

"We see that, for some of you, the vibration of this place is excessive. We have done our best to attenuate it, however. We shall be as brief as possible to minimise this discomfort. In the meantime, greetings and welcome on behalf of the living entity of Ixnor."

Axor looked at Gael and Livingstone, and immediately detected the new bond between them. Deep down, he felt that this was an old bond between travelling souls. So that was one of the reasons why all this was happening. He and Liriel smiled fleetingly at both of them before continuing. Livingstone felt the inner sensation of intense tenderness with profound emotion. He had just received the blessing of the lords of the planet without exchanging a single word with them. At his side, Gael transmitted an identical, joyous feeling to him. Externally, however, he gave nothing away that could be seen by Earth eyes as he felt her thoughts: "This is a landmark in our journey, my dear. Now we are joined again at the deepest levels of our existence."

Then Hamilton Burns answered,

"On behalf of the planet Earth and the United States of America, we greet and thank you for your welcome. Your planet is beautiful and we have greatly enjoyed this first contact. Please accept these gifts as a small token of our esteem."

One of the soldiers stepped forward carrying a metal box and opened it. The Commander took out a small golden statue, a fine example of art nouveau on the planet Earth, a silver box encrusted with precious stones, an example of medieval European jewellery, and an eighteenth century Indian dagger, made of silver, gold and iron, "a weapon of princes", as the Earthman pointed out.

Axor and Liriel thanked him. Yet Livingstone felt that not everything about the gifts had pleased them. Axor spoke up,

"These are interesting examples of your art, my brother. I should like to know one thing about them: why do they have a negative charge and why was this not neutralised?"

Hamilton Burns was stunned.

"I don't understand... What do you mean?"

"I see you are unaware of it, but these objects are partially charged with psychic energy and it is noxious. One of them has taken several human lives and the other two have long been associated with a series of emotions of violence, greed, envy and desire."

"I apologise... I was unaware of any of this. These objects were brought in good faith."

Burns could hardly believe it. True or not, they were undervaluing the gifts. You didn't need to be telepathic to read his unease - it was etched in his face, evident in his slightly raised shoulders. Had they never heard of diplomacy?

"We do not, in any way, wish you to get the impression that we do not appreciate your offering. In fact, it would be easy to neutralise the psychic charge we spoke of. We therefore ask you not to take this request for clarification as ingratitude."

To the navigator it was obvious that offering such presents was an unbelievable mistake. If he had at least known, he might have been able to neutralise the harmful charges. But how could he explain to his fellow Earthmen that the Ixnorians were simply being sincere and loyal and that they, the Earthmen, had done something as unbelievable as offering psychically contaminated objects to such hugely sensitive beings?

Liriel took the floor.

"Before we continue, my brother, I should like you to explain something to me: why do you carry instruments of destruction?"

Burns was taken by surprise. The question was not totally unexpected, though.

"Our weapons are strictly for self-defence. We do not wish to show any aggressive intention by them"

"The possibility that you may need to defend yourselves is merely a mental projection on your part. This planet is entirely safe for you, I can assure you."

Burns was not convinced. He had to be diplomatic, however.

"Thank you. I hope we have caused no offence by bringing weapons."

"No, brother. Let us consider the matter closed. We would like to propose a meeting of minds. If you agree, we shall concentrate deeply and share objectives and knowledge. You shall share knowledge about your journey here, your planet, your ship, your people; we shall share knowledge of our planet, our spirit."

Hamilton Burns looked at Dawson, hesitant, distrustful. It could be a trap. The Ixnorians were trained telepaths and he knew nothing of telepathy. The Commander's response greatly saddened Livingstone, but to Gael it came as no surprise. It was obvious to her that Burns was unable to comprehend the richness of the proposal they were making him. He was also incapable of appreciating the gift of energy that had been given him shortly before by Axor and Liriel or of comprehending that it was the Ixnorian equivalent of a very valuable offer...

"I thank you for the proposal but we are not yet prepared for such a meeting. Let us deliberate on the matter for a few days" (and, to himself: we'll come up with a polite way to refuse).

Axor refrained from ascertaining the real reason for this rejection although he immediately felt the "distortion of inner truth" patent in Hamilton Burns' tone of voice.

"So be it, my brother. May we be of use to you in the meantime?"

"We should like your permission to collect certain minerals from your planet. We are especially interested in certain types of metal and radioactive minerals - we know the subsoil is extremely rich in such substances. We are also aware of the presence of large quantities of diamonds."

Livingstone's blood froze in his veins. He had not been told of this and it could cause serious problems. He had heard and understood Alin's brief comment moments earlier on Dawson's questions. And felt that he himself was little more than an educated primate in comparison to the civilised delicacy of this wonderful people. Axor spoke again.

"What you are saying implies moving minerals from their geomorphic location. We can only agree to such a request after we have learned more about your technicians' studies of the changes this may cause to the vibratory equilibrium of our planet's subsoil. There is one thing we would like to know, however: why do you wish to modify the mineral balance of Ixnor?"

Livingstone realised it would be futile, even dangerous for him to intervene. He was deeply worried and knew that this was not lost on Gael, much less on the wisest beings on Ixnor. He inwardly apologised for the barbarity of his companions. One of the children approached him and gently, wordlessly, stroked one of his hands. At the same time he heard Gael's thought: "Do not worry. Our leaders are aware of the lack of inner luminosity of your companions and can easily handle it. Let us calmly observe what happens."

"I don't believe we can do such a thing. After all, we'd just be taking a few tons of minerals... I'm sure it would be no great loss to you. I'll consult our technicians on the matter, though."

"I believe you should perhaps better evaluate what is at stake. The planet's mineral outcrops are not random occurrences, but obey special designs. They concentrate the energy lines of Ixnor and are their main points of expression and accumulation. May I know the purpose of such a request? Might not the introduction to your world of minerals with specific vibratory characteristics cause some kind of problem?"

What was this? Avarice? Burns was beside himself, all the more so since they obviously seemed to believe that the Earthmen did not know what they were doing. And all this when, far above their heads, they had a giant warship armed to the teeth with enough firepower to reduce this planet to rubble.

"In our world some of these minerals are extremely valuable, others extremely useful". His tone was dry, offended.

"You mean that on the planet Earth you place great value on the simple accumulation of certain classes of mineral? Even if they are not meant for energy purposes?"

"Exactly."

"In that case we ask you to reflect deeply on what you are proposing. If necessary, we shall place our knowledge at your disposal. Such measures may have extremely negative psychic effects on your planet if not properly planned."

The Commander saw this as a tacit refusal, their motives unclear and fanciful, a continuous reference to a superior knowledge which they had yet to demonstrate... The leader was clearly an excellent negotiator. But, if that was so, he too could play the wily old fox...

"Thank you. I would like to return to our mother ship to deliberate on all this. Later some of our technicians may meet with yours."

"Very well. We shall take you to your exploration vessel. In the meantime, any of you are welcome to remain here should you wish to."

Axor was obviously interested in the navigator. But Burns didn't trust him and did not want to leave him there.

"I shall leave three of my men". The Commander turned to three soldiers. "David, Lester, Diana, you'll stay on the planet while we return to the ship."

The navigator opened his mouth to speak.

"But..."

The Commander started to get up, ignoring him. His tone of voice and look clearly signalled the end of the discussion.

"With your permission, we shall now withdraw to our ship".

The next few moments as Livingstone got up, said goodbye, thanked them, and walked the necessary steps to leave the Crystal Star, seemed like a bad dream. He felt bewildered and incredulous, and sensed that something profoundly negative was afoot. Then, as the small ship moved off with Gael inside, whose tenderness he kept within him, the navigator sought to react.

"Commander Burns, I must protest. You should have told me of your interest in the minerals. I also regret that you didn't consult me as to whether I wished to remain on the planet. Don't forget that I am a civilian!"

Burns' retort was dry and blunt. He felt in control once again.

"The objectives of this mission do not concern you. As for the rest, your presence is required on Star 1. In a while I shall discuss your relationship with that girl with you."

The navigator was about to reply, indignant, but was cut off.

"Now is not the time for a discussion. Certain things still need to be done."

Hamilton turned to his second-in-command, Dawson.

"Lieutenant Dawson, quickly collect as many mineral samples as you can. I also want samples of plants, insects and, if possible, some of those birds. And I want to be back on Star 1 in fifteen minutes."

Chapter 12

Minerals, Plants and Animals

As they left the exploration vessel and boarded Star 1, Livingstone was almost exploding with anger and indignation. These fools were risking causing a conflict, the consequences of which were absolutely unpredictable. They had lied to him, deliberately concealing the fact that, perhaps more than any other, the main objective of the mission was economic. They had collected samples of animal, vegetable and mineral life without any consideration for the planetary authorities. They were reacting in a manner that was strangely similar to that adopted centuries before by European explorers in the New World on Earth, when making contact with the inhabitants of a recently discovered land. And, just as before, it was they that were the real savages.

"Commander, I should not only like to vehemently protest at the new manner in which I am being treated, but also point out that you are taking incalculable risks and overstepping the bounds of civility and politeness with the planet Ixnor!"

Hamilton Burns was not concerned. After all, everything pointed to the fact that their technology was, in some aspects, comparable if not superior to that of the Ixnorians. And the latter appeared to have no military resources (not even any police). Besides, the Norya plateau was an isolated spot and no signs of any scanners or humans had been found within many miles of it, just birds, various plants, rocks and a few rodents. He smiled, satisfied.

"Calm down, man! They don't have scanners of any kind in the area; how are they going to find out we took a couple of shrubs, a rodent or two and a few stones?"

"You don't comprehend just how psychically developed they are. They could have been monitoring us all the time without our realising it. And there's the question of principle: what right do we have to take materials from their planet without permission?"

"Listen here, we're not talking about stealing large quantities of minerals or material possessions. We're talking about things that aren't owned by anybody. I don't see what the harm is in removing so little."

"I'll tell you then, in case you're not aware of it, you've just infringed norms which are ethically important for the Ixnorians and for them a thing like that carries great weight! And who are you to decide what's a little or a lot on this planet?"

"And just how do you know all this?"

"Because I had the opportunity to learn from the Interplanetary Welcoming Co-ordinator. And I would have liked to have stayed down there to learn some more. Perhaps you could explain why I wasn't allowed to?"

"You seem to be getting a little too friendly with them; besides, you're of more use to us up here than down there having fun with that girl. And we are in a position of strength. We don't have to go tiptoeing around afraid we might annoy them. If they know so much, maybe they know *that* too!"

"They're not interested in your military strength, I can assure you. But they will start to worry if we continue to behave like primitive apes. See if you've got it straight: we are basically unworthy of being here because we are not yet able to show any decency in relation to peoples from different planets. You have come in the name of the planet Earth and are choosing to portray us as a bunch of savages and thieves!"

The tone of the dialogue went from bad to worse. When the navigator threatened to stop providing his services and when he demanded that the research be stopped, calling the Commander an "archaic anthropoid", the latter drew his own conclusions.

"Lieutenant Dawson, take this man into custody. He is to be considered guilty of insubordination and suspected of carrying out acts of sabotage."

The navigator continued to protest as he sought to attain a state of deep tranquillity that would allow him to respond more appropriately to the situation. Things were spinning out of control, though, and he knew it.

"Listen, Commander: I can try to explain some things to you about the culture you're dealing with. Please don't take any rash decisions. Don't offend beings that have done you no harm. They're more powerful than you can imagine although they seek the ways of peace!"

"For the time being, our conversation is over. Later, when you've calmed down a little, we shall speak again. Until then, may I remind you that your loyalties lie with the planet Earth and not these individuals. Do not forget that any thoughtless act on your part may lead to a summary trial."

A short while later, Hamilton Burns and his technicians sat discussing the characteristics of the biological specimens they had captured and the mapping of the mineral resources of the planet that was being carried out as they orbited Ixnor. Despite the setback caused by the navigator's reaction, he was satisfied with the preliminary report. The planet was incredibly rich in radioactive minerals, metals that were rare on Earth, and diamonds... all easily accessible. Several vegetable and animal specimens had striking structural and cellular similarities with those on Earth. They would soon have the results of their genetic make-up but everything pointed to total compatibility. With luck, they would find elements that were useful for the agricultural and pharmaceutical industries back on Earth. And even if the navigator decided to go all the way with his demands for an immediate end to all research until permission from the planet leaders had been obtained, he wouldn't have to give in. They had taken the precaution of bringing along two extra crew members to substitute Livingstone should he refuse to retranslocate the ship back to Earth.

On the Norya plateau, Twick felt the cry for help of the small captured animals. He watched as the strangely opaque beings carried away birds and rodents, their distress more psychic than physical. He watched them collect a series of small stones from the ground and tear up plants by the root. Twick had no way of understanding; but his joyful albeit nebulous consciousness registered the disharmony and abnormality of the situation. He felt odd without knowing why and even without knowing he felt odd. So when the noisy, frightening ship moved off, blowing up whirlwinds of dust, he remained for a long time curled up in his niche, scared and upset, his slender arms wrapped around his body as if trying to comfort himself. He moaned quietly as a shudder ran through him. Then, sensing a vague need to do so, headed towards the Third City of Water. He had to make contact with the beings that looked on the planet as their garden, the ones that caressed and smiled at living things. Twick was unable to reason in such a clear fashion but he felt the rightness of the need to be with them right now.

A while later, tending to her plants, Luilan noticed the small shape hopping through them towards her. It was rare to find one of the small builders of vegetable forms from the plateau here and she looked at it curiously. Twick seemed agitated, his body trembling, his large eyes reflecting his fear and amazement. The little girl concentrated harder. What she felt had a profound effect on her and she stopped her daily chores at once. It was startling and iniquitous beyond imagination. She had only heard of such things in her "Evolutive Variations in Cosmic Consciousness" classes. She remembered the horrendous descriptions they had been given of the acts carried out by semi-aware human beings in certain pre-cosmic civilisations. Was it possible that there were a horde of them in that huge orbiting spaceship? Whatever the case, she was a citizen of the planet, a normal Ixnorian adolescent. She would do what she had to.

Approximately thirty minutes later, a fast transport vehicle stopped outside the Crystal Star. Luilan was not yet skilled enough to exchange detailed telepathic information with members of the Planetary Council at a distance. Feeling a little embarrassed at the greatness of this wonderful place, she asked for a meeting with "some member of the Council". The watcher on duty, Zultar, looked at her good-naturedly before mentally questioning her. She felt his kindness and compassion, but also his genuine interest in her needs.

"...My sister, I see that you carry the weight of a great burden. Are you sure it deserves the attention of the Planetary Council?"

"...Unfortunately I am certain of it. I have just made contact with a small plant constructor coming from the Norya Plateau and I think that some bad things are happening there. Our Earth visitors have broken the rules of ecological respect..."

The brief mental exchange lasted for only a few moments. Zultar's face took on a determined look. If Livingstone were there he would have recognised the Fire of Will burning in those clear, benevolent eyes which now flashed like steel. The young girl was speaking the complete truth. It was almost unthinkable that a visitor would dare to infringe the elementary norms of interplanetary fellowship. The matter had to be looked into urgently as he sensed an approaching crisis, one that would require the adoption of security measures.

"...I shall act at once on what you have told me. Please wait a few moments in the council chamber. And, my sister (he smiled, his kind air restored as he himself restored her in the peace of mind that flows through the inner ways of itself)...I am grateful for your diligence."

Zultar strode quickly away. At the same time, he made contact with the Council.

Aila, the Ethics Officiant, arrived a few moments later in the hearing room. She greeted Luilan with the fan-shaped gesture of her hand, spreading the energy of truth and balance, and stood in front of the adolescent, gazing into her eyes. Communication flowed quickly between them in a crystal-clear exchange of feelings and thoughts.

Luilan described the circumstances in which she had found Twick, how disturbed the small creature was and her attempts to help it with all her love as she sought to discover the reason for its unease. That was when she had understood. Before boarding their ship, which had emitted such profoundly discordant sounds, the Earthmen had captured various birds and rodents and placed them in cages. By doing so, they had shown complete insensitivity to the anguish caused to imprisoned living beings. They had accused them of nothing nor made any mental declaration about their acts. The reason for capturing them seemed strangely obscure. They had removed mineral and animal specimens from the area without making any request to do so and without assessing the impact this would have on the psychic environment. They had apparently failed to take into account the negative biomagnetic disturbance they were causing and the fact that they were interfering with the psychic mechanisms of the small animals and insects in the area. They had not even consulted the Administrators of Nature. As if they weren't even aware of their existence and had no idea of the work of creation, alignment and constant adjustment of the standard patterns underlying mineral and vegetable life that these carried out.

A short while later the hearing came to an end. Aila embraced and kissed Luilan, smiling, and spoke for the first time.

"Thank you, dear sister, for your diligence. I take the weight of this event from your shoulders. From here on, the Council will take charge and act accordingly. You may return to your rhythm of life in peace. May the Light of the Cosmos continue to inspire you."

The young adolescent, now bathed in tranquil gratitude, returned home, relieved, as the Planetary Council briefly pondered the matter.

Hamilton Burns had just finished discussing the on-going investigation into Ixnor's natural resources when he was informed that Axnor had appeared on their video monitors - and nobody quite knew how - requesting immediate contact with the Commander. He turned on his monitor, somewhat surprised. There was the calm face of that strange individual, one that looked so young yet had the voice of an ageless wise man.

"My brother, you and your companions have removed several animals, vegetables and minerals from our planet without any consideration for the suffering of living, conscious specimens and without evaluating the psychic and vibratory disturbance that this has brought about. You have done this without seeking prior authorisation and have thus disobeyed the rules of ecological respect. I ask you: are we to interpret this as a deliberate act of aggression? Are you aware that you are acting on a level that has long been surpassed by those that see the Universe as a place of sharing?"

Burns was not expecting this. Yet he still felt confident in his role, surrounded as he was by the gigantic metal panels of his ship, by his soldiers and technicians, by powerful weapons.

"Axor, I can assure you that it is not, in any way, our intention to carry out hostile acts against the Ixnorians. We have merely removed an infinitesimal sample of your mineral, animal and vegetable kingdoms for research purposes."

"If all you seek is information, you may ask whatever questions you like of our technicians. In the meantime, I ask you to free the imprisoned animals and replace the plants and minerals you have taken back on the surface of Ixnor. Such a gesture would, for us, clear up any misunderstanding..."

"I'm afraid that is not feasible."

"Could you explain your position better?"

"Some of the rodents we took have died and have been dissected. Something similar is happening with the plants and even some of the mineral samples. I am truly sorry but we never thought that this would cause offence. My formal apologies."

Axor was in possession of nearly all the information necessary for that moment.

"My brother, your apologies do not ring sincere. I believe that you are lying and that you deliberately ordered this crime to be committed in order to avoid having to return the specimens. May I know the real reason for your behaviour?"

Damn telepath! It was going to be difficult dealing with him. Burns was already sufficiently annoyed, what with the "fraternal" treatment and everything, but was not entirely insensitive to the worrying ease with which Axor had appeared on the monitors nor the fact that he had absolutely no idea how he had discovered everything. He decided to change his approach. His strategy of presenting consummated facts with an air of ingenuity was not working.

"Very well, it is true that I gave the order for the immediate study of the specimens we collected. The reason for this has to do with why we came here. On the planet Earth, it cost huge amounts of money to construct this ship; we had hoped to bring back some minerals and, perhaps, biological species that would help pay for it and, if possible, demonstrate that this adventure was worth it. Mainly because some of the minerals we are interested in are very rare on Earth, yet extremely important for the preparation of precision instruments or the production of energy. I hope you understand that we are here at the service of our planet."

"Does this mean, then, that on your planet you trade biological life for material possessions?"

"I don't understand the question."

"The way we see it, what you are telling me is extremely worrying. It appears that, for yourselves, the planetary economy is dependent on the accumulation of minerals and that this is considered sufficiently important to justify the death of living beings. Even if this death is brought about cruelly and does not respect the cycle of life..."

"That's partly the case, yes, but remember that our intention is to make these small deaths useful for many human beings."

"I must warn you that your customs and ethics seem unworthy of interstellar travellers. Please consider this carefully and do not remove any more Ixnorian specimens. Such behaviour seriously offends us and shows a lack of respect for cosmic life. And please shorten your visit."

"Let's say I respect this request in relation to animals and plants. Could we not, as a compromise, say, remove minerals which for us are precious?"

"What I said at our first meeting still holds true. The matter must be carefully evaluated by yours and our technicians, and will depend on the nature of the minerals, their location and their role in the planet's biomagnetic system. However, I fail to understand how you can speak of 'compromise' in relation to our request."

"Let's just say we could try to find a middle ground..."

Axor was now entirely certain that this being Burns did not seek to align himself with the flow of the Cosmos. On the contrary, he obeyed an apparent semi-chaos of badly managed personal forces. He (and probably most of the Earth newcomers) still put their own personal interests and the acquisition of material possessions first. A kind of thief of the Cosmos, interested in obtaining benefits for himself rather than in the idea of giving, which nourishes freedom and growth. He had not come to Ixnor to learn and to give, in an exchange of minds, but to seize different physical materials to serve his apparent self-centred animal nature. The contrast with Ixnorian ethics was absolute. On Ixnor, the worth of each individual depended on their capacity to work, to provide wisdom, psychic energy... The Ixnorians would rather die than betray other forms of life in any way. And then these Earthmen arrived, capable of betraying life itself simply to obtain benefits for themselves and the most material and blunted level of their existence...

Yet they had brought an unmistakably different being along with them. At least one, perhaps more. He felt this was the case.

"Brother, I shall now interrupt this dialogue. Your proposal is, for us, senseless. All we ask is that you respect our laws and, above all, the Law of the Cosmos. I ask you to consider this fact and make contact with us again shortly. In the meantime, I would like you to send your navigator to us so we can clear things up."

The very idea was unthinkable. This was becoming decidedly suspicious. Livingstone was the last person he would send down to the planet, despite his good relationship with Gael, before making sure of his loyalty.

"I regret to inform you he is temporarily unavailable. His insubordination has landed him in custody. Perhaps this will be possible soon, though."

"My brother, it is quite possible that you are committing an injustice..."

That was too much.

"I'm sorry, Axor, but I will not tolerate any interference on your part in our internal affairs. He is none of your business!"

Hamilton Burns obviously believed he could manipulate animal and human lives at will. The supreme leader of Ixnor could foresee a good many of the events that would unfold and the alternative to each. The lines of time stretched out clearly before him and all pointed to the withdrawal of the Earthmen and a return to their home planet within a few days.

"Even so, you are still making a mistake. For now, I shall leave you to make your own decisions. I shall await further contact from you. Do you agree?"

"I do. I shall contact you in three days."

Sitting in his quarters, two guards outside the door, Livingstone was quite calm. There was nothing to do but wait. So he remained silent, mindful of what was going on, sounding out his consciousness in search of the right path to follow. It was then that he felt the inner touch of Axor's vibration.

"...My brother, I know of your present state and your concern. You must wait in peace, however. We know you have nothing to do with the events that are taking place and that you will not be implicated when they reach their epilogue..."

A brief telepathic contact that left him totally calm and joyful. He must wait, no doubt about it. The Ixnorians were too wise for him to even imagine that his worries were worth worrying about. And perhaps they even knew how to react to the military threat. It was evident to him that the Ixnorians were aware of the destructive power of the Earth ship and that it didn't bother them. He just didn't know why...

Chapter 13

Diana

The city seemed to be in her skin, in her bones, in her nervous system. And it made her feel strangely well. Diana, a Star 1 officer, was enchanted by every nook and cranny of the City of Water as she walked through it, a little mystified at the open, friendly welcome she received from all those she met. They treated her as if they were old friends, with an unexpected carefreeness, after all, she had journeyed from the other end of the universe; shouldn't they at least be more cautious? Noticing a carefully sculpted bench in a pleasant area of the city, she stopped and sat down. She felt the need for reflection. In front of her, enormous sprays of high-pressure water crossed in the middle of a meadow, splitting the Ixnorian sunlight into numerous flashes of colour.

Diana had been present during the exchange between the Commander and the planet leaders, and had not enjoyed the way things had gone at all. She had felt a mixture of pity and fear at the way the dialogue had unfolded; it was not her place to argue with the Commander, however, nor to question orders. Even if she had thought it unfair and odd that the navigator had been forced to return to the ship, when she had the impression he would be of far greater use on Ixnor. And besides, the young girl had taken to Henry Livingstone. He was an interesting individual, immensely knowledgeable about the human mind and physically attractive to boot. He was a mature man, in his fifties and in excellent shape. Grey hair but an unwrinkled face, his muscular body indicative of someone who looked after his physique. She was also keen on martial arts although it was not her strong point. But what she appreciated most in the man was the manner in which he had borne the responsibility of translocating the ship and its crew and carried it through with consummate perfection.

The young officer had received intense training, taking full advantage of her obvious abilities, to prepare her to substitute Livingstone should it prove necessary. She had passed numerous tests, both physically and psychologically demanding. These included situations in which different people attempted to find out to what extent she was able to conceal the real reason for her inclusion on the Star 1 journey. Sometimes they asked unexpected, insinuating questions to try and catch her out, on other occasions they claimed they had been briefed on the mission details and wanted to exchange opinions with her about it. She had passed all these tests with flying colours, following her instructions to the letter: "Except when expressly ordered to do so by Commander Burns or his second-in-command Lieutenant Dawson, you shall not discuss any aspect of this mission with anyone - and that includes civilian and military personnel." Indeed, they had made it clear to her that this was a top-secret mission and, deep down, she liked the idea. It somehow made her feel important. Diana had been a rebellious teenager, alienated by her parents' divorce and various other ups and downs, and had looked on a military career as a way of leaving her mother's home with greater ease. At the time, one of her ambitions had been to lead an independent life, to be with whoever she wanted to. She liked to wear her hair short, too, and to take by surprise those rare men that tried to "take advantage of the fragile young girl" - although she was reasonably attractive. She had once sent one to the hospital after an unsuccessful attempt at a slightly-too-forward kiss. And yet she liked to feel feminine and to be caressed, although she could only sometimes let these feelings come to the fore. There was something else that had always followed her, too: she was something of a dreamer and possessed certain paranormal abilities. She was never one to set much stock on metaphysical speculation but, even so, things sometimes happened to her that she was unable to explain to herself and therefore unable to explain to others. In the army they had only learnt of these facts from her response to an enquiry. That had started things off...

She remembered, years before, sitting on the edge of a lake watching a group of ducks - which she had hitherto hunted with great success: Diana was an excellent shot and proud of it. Then she had heard the crack of a gun and seen one of the birds fall from the sky, thudding to the ground a few metres away. She had got up to look at the animal as she waited for the hunter that had shot it to arrive, when suddenly she noticed its expression. The animal was still alive. In a flash, she felt its emotional distress, the incredible desolation of this creature unable to comprehend the sudden passage from awareness of the wind in its feathers, the clarity, the flock with which it was flying, to the spinning descent and intense pain. When he arrived, the hunter found her crying bitterly, the duck, now dead, in her hands. He was incapable of claiming his trophy and moved off without a word.

What had led her to remember that day with such intensity? Years had passed and she only remembered it as a demonstration of her extrasensory powers. Use of them had never again been as painful. Perhaps, in the City of Water, the atmosphere of sensitivity and beauty had tuned her in to the memory of the lake upon whose banks she had spent so many enjoyable moments...

First and foremost, Diana was an army officer on a mission (albeit a low ranking one, she thought, amused). She knew that she had not been chosen to remain on the planet by chance and that Commander Hamilton Burns trusted her to obtain an accurate report on the mentality of the Ixnorians and, perhaps, what it was that they were planning. She was finding it hard to play such a role, however. She felt as if she was walking in disguise in a world of genuine people. She was unable to think in military or strategic terms and, to make things worse, found herself enjoying it. She found she liked everyone. Then came the worry as she remembered her mission: was she getting soft? Was she being submitted to some strange telepathic influence that was countering her training? Was it all some clever trick, her intimate reaction to the Ixnorians a sham, they themselves ship hunters or something? Images from old Earth science fiction movies came to mind; the baddies - the aliens, of course - equipped with unsuspected weapons hidden in caves which were suddenly taken out and used. Not to mention aliens that could manipulate minds, aliens that devoured Earthmen and dozens of other threats dreamed up by screenwriters. Suddenly, Diana remembered that there *she* was the alien, an extra-Ixnorian life form, and it was her ship that was a threat to the planet. She almost fell over with the shock as the thought struck her inner perception working feverishly from then on. For several long, anguished moments, she questioned everything: herself, the mission, even whether they should be there at all. The warlike behaviour of the Commander and many of the Star 1 crew was in stark contrast to the tenderness which seemed to emanate from the whole planet. She looked to one side and saw a small group of Ixnorians looking at her affectionately. One of them, an attractive dark-haired youngster, spoke to her.

"Forgive us, my sister, but we were passing by and noticed your expression. We do not wish to bond to you without your first expressing an interest to do so, but we feel you are in great discomfort. May we be of assistance?"

Diana didn't know what to say. She couldn't very well accuse them of interfering since they had not only deliberately remained at a greater distance than they usually kept between themselves, but had also merely shown a calm willingness to help. They irradiated kindness and peace of mind. She could in no way discuss what she felt with them, though. On the contrary, her ingrained sense of prudence and loyalty to the Earthmen came to the fore.

"Thank you for your concern. I'm fine... I mean, I will be. I was just thinking of my planet. Don't worry."

The small group said farewell and moved off. It was obvious to her that they realised she was not being entirely sincere but even so had respected her evident need to be alone.

Diana sat down in a corner close to a small fountain surrounded by grass and plants, and remained there, letting the crystalline sound and the soft wind help her straighten out her thoughts. She must not neglect her mission nor forget Earth's interests. Basically, the Commander's main aim was to safeguard them. Why, then, was she unable to convince herself that the position they had adopted was the correct one?

The young officer felt like crying, even if this wasn't much of a military thing to do. Even if she wanted to try to act differently rather than merely complete her mission, she didn't know how. What was left? A court martial, then prison or something worse? Besides, she still hoped to return to Earth a heroine, someone that had made an important contribution to the success of the first interstellar journey ever undertaken by Earthmen. With this thought uppermost in her mind, she tried to feel grateful to her superiors. And almost succeeded.

When the young man that had spoken to her earlier approached her again, she reacted with some surprise. What did he have to say now? Now that everything seemed a little calmer...

"Excuse me, sister. I have returned because I sense that you are still ill at ease. I do not wish to intrude on your inner world but, if you wish, I would like to invite you to a concert. It's not far from here."

She thought for a moment. She recalled how fond she had been of going to concerts back on Earth, especially during her rebellious youth. Music that transmitted raw emotion and a tremendous desire for freedom. Protest music, music that spoke of love and sex, music that spoke of drugs, but also poets that found inspiration in something more than fantastic projections under the effect of acid.

"Thank you. I'd love to go. I'm quite curious, actually. Would you lead the way?"

She accompanied him for a few minutes, half lost in thought. He walked by her side, smiling but highly respectful of her "telepathic silence".

The hall where the concert was to take place was an odd, goblet shape. A huge goblet made of dark stones that appeared extremely hard, with no seams or differences in colour. Overhead was a transparent crystal dome of equally impressive dimensions. As she entered, Diana knew that everyone there was aware that she was an extra-Ixnorian. But the atmosphere was at once welcoming, warm and refreshing. Smiles played over the faces of those that were looking at her although, to be honest, most didn't seem to pay her much attention.

She sat down on a chair next to the young man that had invited her. The chair was large with carefully prepared armrests, and seemed to have been anatomically designed to provide maximum comfort. It was made of a brilliant metal with cushioned areas composed, as far as she could tell, of some sort of vegetable fibre. She could have sworn that there were no synthetic polymers anywhere in the room. She settled down. Smiling, she asked the young man next to her - who had introduced himself as Tumir - to explain what was going on.

"I would prefer not to nourish your mind with any expectations. What I can tell you is that there will be sounds and colours and that the musicians will appear in a few moments. Do you see those shapes? That's where they'll play."

Diana looked where he had pointed and saw what looked like various bowls of different shapes and sizes (the largest must have been ten metres in diameter). They appeared to be made of rock crystal or something similar. She then saw various musicians, carrying what must have been instruments, climb up into some of the bowls and settle down. There were what looked like bells, instruments that looked like xylophones, what may have been drums, and large crystal shapes that could have been horns... although she didn't see how they could be played. Some had nothing but themselves, which led her to conclude they were singers. Then the different shaped bowls and their occupants rose into the air and hung there, quite still, at different heights and at different points in the hall. At the centre of the hanging crystal dome a light came and began to spin slowly round in a clockwise direction, its rays striking a glass pyramid directly below it and producing extraordinarily beautiful reflections of colours. And silence fell.

The musicians began to play, apparently all at the same time; yet the sound only gradually, gently increased in volume, quicker in some places, slower in others, as Diana felt herself plunge into a world of unimaginable sounds. There were basic rhythms interwoven with melodies composed of soft variations of continuous sounds, the splash of cymbals (or something similar), sounds of the wind and crystal, sounds of stone, sounds of water, the trilling of birds, suggestions of what may have been the wind rustling in the trees... The music seemed to progressively fill the hall, penetrating bones, bodies, veins, even the very air breathed by those present. Even the chairs responded to the chords, vibrating in response, while the huge stone bowl that was the base of the hall also responded to the echoes that rang out from the gigantic crystal bell-glass high overhead... Diana closed her eyes. She felt herself floating in a universe of shimmering, glittering lights, a universe of sounds that had the consistency of translucent, coloured shapes, a universe of lights that seemed to resonate as they shone... The sound died down to a level that was almost below the threshold of her perception. Then, quite unexpectedly, the musician in the largest bowl in the middle of the hall struck what appeared to be some sort of gong while, in various places, powerful male and female voices, purer than anything Diana had ever heard, chanted continuously, a sound that reminded her of the OM she had heard several times on Earth at meditation groups and some rock concerts.

Without knowing how, she felt something within her spiral upwards and found herself floating several metres above her chair. She looked down. Her body was still sitting there. There were lots of bodies sitting in seats. Next to her, however, there were many beings, similar to the bodies, which seemed to be dancing in the lights and in the sounds, indescribably happy, vibrating with the music, they themselves giving off waves of light in response, they themselves singing... And she felt a part of them and found herself dancing in the air as well. Her body, a few metres below, wept in response to the emotion but also to one thought, which she felt sharp and clear... The music spoke of the Cosmos and of Love. A love song for gods and goddesses, a harmony of sounds made to express the way in which the galaxies consciously communicate... And all was sound, all was movement, all was love that moved from the tiniest of particles to the largest galactic masses. The Universe was like that love song. Under the dome, each found their sound in the song. Under the Universe, too...

When Diana left - how much later she didn't know - she was no longer the same. She felt light, luminous, joyful, pure. And she couldn't help but laugh at herself and her reluctant, distrustful attitude when she had landed on this blessed planet. There could be no malice in people capable of creating such art. And that was an understatement.

Chapter 14

The Incident

The day following the communication between Star 1 and Axor, Lester was sitting comfortably in his individual room in the City of Water when the Interplanetary Welcoming Co-ordinator appeared. He couldn't help but admire the beauty of the woman, the body that was easily imaginable beneath her light, unpretentious clothes. She made him yearn for the women he had had relationships with back on Earth, reminding him of so many games of seduction, so many hours of fun - and the admiration that a reasonable number of casual companions had felt for his masculine abilities. Wasn't it worth trying his luck with her? He had been given no orders to the contrary and it might even prove useful, even more so since she had already shown an interest in one Earthman and he had been removed from the competition, he thought, satisfied with his cunning.

As always, despite the fact that she felt an unpleasant effect from Lester's body, one that was manifestly disharmonious, almost nauseous in terms of his biomagnetism, Gael was careful not to make telepathic contact with the man without first feeling the corresponding sensitivity and readiness on his part. The Ixnorians took great care in this respect and she would never want to hurt his feelings by telepathically declaring to him, with the blunt sincerity typical of Ixnor, that his body was full of toxins and therefore incapable of "expressing the musicality of health" or that his aura was strangely dull and ugly... What sense would this make to an Earthman whose thoughts, emotions and physique were out of balance and who was used to feeding his body with dead animals? Besides, although she was well aware of the earlier physical and psychic actions of the Earthmen, she did not want to prejudge the three Earthmen that had remained on the surface. The stance adopted by their commander did not necessarily make them dishonest creatures.

"Good morning, brother. I hope you had a restful night."

"Good morning, Gael. Thank you for asking. To what do I owe the pleasure of your visit?"

"I just came to find out if you are enjoying your stay on our planet and to see if there's anything I can do for you."

She had sat down in a chair facing him, smiling, awaiting his answer. Lester thought she might perhaps fancy him. After all, on Earth when a woman walked into a man's quarters and sat down in front of him with a smile on her face, it usually meant something. Satisfied that was probably the answer, he gazed into her eyes and thought he saw an inviting glint.

"Actually, I would like to get to know you better."

Gael noticed with her clairvoyant look that the Earthman's lower energy centres were becoming quite active. She also felt the irradiation from his genital centre in an extremely unpleasant way. She saw trouble on the horizon.

"What would you like to know about me?"

He moved a little closer. This was going well. Maybe the Ixnorians went in for sex in a big way. The idea vaguely occurred to him that soon he might be rolling around in bed with her. After all, he was a fine male specimen. And she was nothing to spit at. Why not go for it?

"I want to know everything. I want to know your full name, how you spend your days, what you do to have fun."

He winked at Gael, hoping for some encouraging sign in return. Gael felt in the wink and the psychic emanation that accompanied it a manifestation of sexual primitivism that was inconceivable to her, despite the explanations Livingstone had given her. The man was still governed by instinctive manifestations akin to the sexual displays of the common animal kingdom... She was responsible for welcoming those that visited her planet, however, and could not help feeling sorry for him and his naive animality. Lester was like an Ixnorian child in an adult body, the problem being that in comparison to the latter he was sensorially deficient. He could only pick up the narrowest band of the vast range of vibratory irradiations that were normally seen and heard by younger Ixnorians. So she smiled almost maternally, which was taken as another good sign by Lester.

"My name is simply Gael. For us, what's important in a name is the reverberation of the sound and the psychic effect it produces and expresses."

"But it's a pretty name. It has a lovely sound to it... And what do you do for fun? You do have places where you can have fun, don't you?"

"It depends what you mean by fun. One of the ways I enjoy spending the time I have available is contemplating sound."

Contemplating sound? Didn't they know what it was to dance to a funky rhythm on this planet? Lester didn't particularly like the way the conversation was going but wanted to come across as kind.

"That sounds interesting. Do you want to tell me how you do it?"

She clearly felt the gulf between them and the fact that they were talking on completely different levels. His magnetism was obviously targeted at her body, as if nothing else existed. She had the feeling that he viewed her as an empty body, energyless and soulless. Gael could speak to him about the meaning of contemplating sound and the doors to a heightened state of consciousness that this opened; but it would be like asking a bird to understand the technical aspects involved in constructing a group of buildings integrated into the landscape. And birds were not equipped to deal with the morphological subtleties of the landscape nor the lines of force underlying natural geometry...

"Oh, it probably wouldn't interest you. Why not tell me about yourself?"

Gael was already more than convinced that prolonging this interchange would be a useless waste of energy and may lead to various misunderstandings. Lester showed signs of a primitivism worthy of the human inhabitants of Ixnor a good 5000 years ago... And yet he had traversed Space on a journey that was, in principle, unfeasible for pre-cosmic civilisations.

The Earthman took this as another positive sign. Maybe she was the shy type and preferred to talk about him rather than herself.

"Well, what can I tell you? I'm an adventurer from my planet, but I'm also a man who appreciates a pretty woman no matter where she is. I never thought I'd meet someone like you here. You make me miss Earth women but, at the same time, I'm glad I'm with you."

His concept of beauty as something merely physical did not go unnoticed by Gael. The Interplanetary Welcoming Co-ordinator was increasingly aware of the latent threat. The frustration of erotic designs centred exclusively on the physical body was one of the things which could cause the primitive inhabitants of Ixnor, thousands of years ago, to become violent. She was unable to lie, however. All she could do was be cautious in expressing the truth. Besides, she felt an obligation to admit that perhaps it was possible to help that soul expand, at least, its perception.

"Thank you for your kind words. Yet I feel that your idea of beauty is connected only with the exterior body. Am I wrong?"

"I don't understand. I'm telling you I find you pretty the way I see you."

"You only see a tiny part of me. As if I were judging your whole body by just a few hairs."

This was a hard one to crack all right! Timid yet openly kind. Maybe he should try a different approach. Perhaps she was the maternal type? Lester stood up slowly, as if to show her something, then pretended to trip, fall and hurt his leg. Gael quickly got up and moved towards him, anxious to check his physical condition. But she immediately felt something was not right. His tone of voice...

"Did you hurt yourself?"

"Not really..." (Lester pretended to be in pain as she held his leg and examined it).

A few moments later, the Co-ordinator looked deep into his eyes.

"Brother, you have no kind of superficial or internal injury. My conclusion is that either you are lying about your condition or have suffered some sort of brain damage."

He felt like a child caught with its hand in the cookie jar, which annoyed him intensely. This resulted in an emission of biomagnetic energy that, once again, was not lost on Gael. Out of politeness, she still held on to the notion that he may have a brain problem.

"Me? Lie? Are you sure there's nothing wrong? My leg really hurts..."

"Your leg is fine. Let me examine your head."

The gesture was pointless since it was obvious, even without resorting to telepathy, that he had lied. The likelihood that he had suffered some kind of brain damage that would cause him to feel such pain was practically nil. Even so, Gael preferred to take his word as far as she could. She moved closer and gently placed her hands around Lester's head. He interpreted this as a caress, even more so since she was giving off an extremely pleasant warmth. He reached out his arm and wrapped it around her waist.

Gael reacted immediately. Her voice became dry and imperative.

"Move your hand. Now."

Lester didn't understand. Had he misinterpreted her movements? Or maybe this was one of the little games the Ixnorian played... He left his arm where it was.

"Hey, now. I didn't want to offend you. It's just that you're so attractive..."

Gael couldn't stand another second of his odorous discharge, his crude, clumsy attempt at approximation. The invasion of her aura, his attempt at emotional coercion, were more than she had ever thought she might one day experience. She focused her psychic energy, diluting it slightly so as not to be too aggressive. And deliberately used words to exteriorise it.

"MOVE AWAY!"

Her voice was only a little louder than usual. For Lester, though, it sounded like various thousand watt speakers had been turned on right next to his ear. He was pushed backwards, overwhelmed by a feeling of violent anguish. Shaking his head, sitting on the floor and feeling incredibly weak, he stared at Gael. She stood in front of him, impassively. Her affable, available air had returned.

Slowly getting to his feet, Lester spoke to her, irritated, angry and afraid.

"What did you do to me? What kind of a witch are you?"

"I pushed you away. May I remind you that you must respect all the citizens of this planet and that we are against all forms of psychic pressure exercised on human beings. You just broke our rules."

"You'll pay for this. I'm here as a representative of the Planet Earth. Don't think you can simply do what you did to me and get away with it."

"I did what I had to and I am at peace with myself. As for you, please reflect carefully before channelling your aggression towards me. I have nothing against you but fear that you have treated me in a manner that is unacceptable by our standards."

"What is it with you people? What are you, a bunch of hysterics? You were coming on to me then suddenly attacked me with some sort of trick."

"I ask you again to reflect carefully. I showed no sexual interest in you. I simply treated you with the kindness and care worthy of a representative of another planet."

"And I'm telling you I was attacked! I'm going back to my ship for a full medical. God help you if it shows up any injuries. You don't know who you're dealing with!"

Gael smiled calmly, despite the strange feeling it gave her to see an adult, an apparently quite normal human being that was able to travel the Cosmos, giving in to such childish displays. His aura gave off red and grey flashes. A deplorable business.

"I believe you are emotionally out of control. It would therefore be best to give you some time to compose yourself. If you wish, I will see to it that you are escorted quickly back to your vessel."

"Thanks, Gael, but I'd rather you took me back to the Finder 3 landing site. I'll do the rest."

Gael left after bidding Lester farewell. A few minutes later, Alin appeared to drive him back to the Norya Plateau.

The Earthman had been expecting half a dozen Ixnorians, maybe armed, and wasn't quite sure what they would do to him. Just this woman, smiling as if nothing unusual was taking place. As he left the building where he had stayed, he still felt angry but also apprehensive. Incredulous, he looked around: nobody was paying him any attention except Alin. Somehow it increased his distrust.

"Where are we going, Alin?"

"To the Norya Plateau, my brother. Wasn't that where you told Gael you wanted to go?"

"Well... yes. Yes, it was." He tried to regain the initiative, his tone threatening. "I'm going to call my ship. My commander's going to hear what you did to me!"

She responded with relative politeness, although her facial expression had hardened. It was not easy for Alin to totally overlook the outrage committed by Lester against a planet authority and a close friend.

"I hope you try to be honest when writing your report. You know very well that you acted hastily and without thinking."

"Not at all. It's not my fault that you're all hysterical. We'll see what happens. If I were you, I'd be less calm. I'm an Earth officer and cannot be treated like that!"

They boarded the ship in silence. By the time they reached the plateau, only half a dozen words had passed between them. Alin sensed that it was useless to waste energy on a human being in such a state of emotional imbalance; as for Lester, he was resentful and irritated, but also afraid of saying too much...

Thirty minutes or so later, Commander Burns was talking on the vidcom with Sergeant Lester Morland.

"Very well, Lester: what happened exactly? I want to know precisely how this occurred. I wouldn't want to have you arrested for perjury on a mission of such importance."

"It's like I say, Commander. I don't know what she did to me, but I think it was some sort of... Some sort of spell. I felt dizzy, sick, I was thrown backwards and she just stood there in front of me without saying a word. Then she smiled at me as if making fun. Maybe you should ask our navigator there what it was his little piece of skirt did to me. Maybe he knows."

"Wait a minute: are you claiming she attacked you using psychic force? Just because you had your arm around her waist while she stroked your head?"

"Exactly, Commander. I'll be damned if I'm lying. I think she just changed her mind and got scared or something. She's probably one of those women that like to tease men then hightail it."

"And you did nothing else? You're sure?"

"Well, I threatened her. I said she hadn't heard the last of it."

"Not good. That wasn't such a good idea. After all, we're just visitors to a planet that has so far treated us very well. How did she react, anyway?"

"She treated me like a kid. Said I needed time to compose myself and that if I wanted she'd have me taken back to the ship."

"That's all? She didn't apologise or anything? She didn't say anything else?"

"No. She sent someone else, Alin, to pick me up and that was all."

"Very well. Finder 3 will be there in six minutes. When you return I want you to have a thorough medical check-up. Then I want a detailed report. That's all."

Burns turned off the vidcom. In a way, he had reasons to be pleased. Leaving an impulsive individual like Lester on the planet surface had been worth it. He had given him a reason for protesting to the Ixnorian governmental entities, which suited him just fine. After all, he could now claim that one of his men had been mistreated and that such an act of aggression warranted, at the very least, an immediate apology. And that Gael had failed to realise the misunderstanding her actions were giving rise to and had not reacted properly. He felt on the verge of regaining the upper hand after the relative shock caused by the conversation with Axor and it made him feel good. He also had objective reasons for appearing offended and, perhaps, for intimidating the Ixnorians. The means by which Gael had driven Lester away were unknown, however. Although he really didn't want to, he needed to consult the navigator.

"Lieutenant Dawson, please bring Livingstone to me. I need to talk to him. Tell him that if he wants his detention to come to an end, he'd best co-operate."

Livingstone was seriously worried. Not only did he feel that something terrible was afoot, he also had reasons to believe that Gael had been involved in some particularly undesirable events. Deep down he felt calm but his thoughts were at fever pitch. He had to decide how to proceed. Perhaps there was still hope that the commander would come to his senses. Perhaps he could be made aware of the ethics of the situation if he could explain them clearly enough to him. At the same time, though, the navigator felt that events were unfolding as if obeying a specific logic. Most worrying of all was the fact that he didn't understand this logic and had no way of predicting whether it would lead to catastrophe. And a catastrophe seemed a possibility.

At that moment two soldiers opened the door and Lieutenant Dawson stepped in. He smiled at the navigator, genuinely. After all, he didn't entirely share the Commander's point of view, given his sensitivity to anthropological issues. Different cultures needed to be respected.

"Livingstone, the Commander wishes to see you. Be careful what you say and try to co-operate. If you're helpful, you may be released from detention."

Later, on the bridge, Livingstone was briefed on the events as they had been described. Inside, he felt a succession of unusual and undesirable feelings that he tried to suppress as each arose. Amazement, jealousy, indignation, anguish, succeeding and overlapping each other. It was imperative that he control his emotions without allowing them to cloud his powers of concentration and discerning judgement. What was at stake was far more than just his personal well-being. On the other hand, it was obvious that Lester was only aware of what his befuddled mind was capable of understanding. Which was not a lot...

"Commander, I believe that Sergeant Lester acted in a manner that dishonours all of us. I suggest that he be suitably punished and that the Ixnorians be informed."

"I'll be the one to decide that. It's not your place to suggest to me what I should or shouldn't do. There's something else I want from you: what do you think happened? What weapon did the Co-ordinator use?"

"I don't think she used any sort of weapon. If I you want my opinion, she legitimately defended herself by projecting the necessary psychic force to get the sergeant away from her. She didn't just attack him out of the blue, and she didn't injure him at all. She was just defending her integrity."

"Psychic force? You mean they can use their mental powers against us?"

"I'm sure they can. But they won't. Not against us and never as an act of aggression."

"What makes you say that?"

"The fact that they hold the right to life as something extremely precious and have a great sense of justice. In case you haven't noticed yet, Commander, they are not aggressive. They may try to defend themselves if attacked, but they won't do anything to this ship on their own initiative."

"Well, I'll have you know I intend to demand a formal apology from them for having been excessive in their treatment of Lester."

Livingstone felt a chill run down his spine. Burns was about to set out in search of conflict and it was obvious he was doing it deliberately to take advantage of his strength. He managed to remain calm, though. He breathed in deeply, relaxed his body and, inside, adopted a non-resistant emotional state, while at the same time avoiding any cerebral tension. He left the personal level and entered into contact with his "inner I". Then, attempting to irradiate tranquillity and discretion, spoke again.

"That seems an unjustified position to adopt. We have to understand that they are not governed by Earth standards."

"I'm sorry, but you're the one that doesn't seem to understand. This is politics. Whether it's ultimately fair or not doesn't interest me. They have given me the chance to act and that's what I'm going to do. It's not only our prestige that's at stake, it's the need we have for the minerals on Ixnor, Earth's need for them."

"Commander, I don't care if you have me arrested again, but what you're saying is monstrous. You make us seem like a bunch of thieves coming from the other side of the Galaxy. And you're treating them in a way that's unknown to them because it's so low and primitive. From their point of view, you're acting like little more than an animal. Please do not dishonour mankind even further. Don't give them the idea that we sent a clever animal along as an ambassador. Don't be that clever animal!"

"Livingstone... I do believe you have crossed the line. I shall do as you wish and let you meditate some more."

The Commander turned to Dawson.

"Lieutenant Dawson, please escort Dr. Livingstone back to his quarters. He is to remain in detention."

Chapter 15

Scrutiny

The Planetary Council of Ixnor was once more in session. A decision had to be reached on the measures to adopt given the development of recent events. The Crystal Star vibrated with the deliberations of the guardians of Ixnorian humanity, irradiating a powerful blue light that could be clearly seen even from afar. In the echo of their minds, the planet's leaders made their feelings known and quickly reached a mutual decision. Once more, the Dome of Unification was the nerve centre, the focal point of constructive or, if necessary, destructive activity. These synchronised minds would never opt for measures aimed at taking the lives of the Earthmen, however. There was total agreement on this based, in turn, on their total respect and affection for the lives of living beings. Nevertheless, it had become necessary to foresee in detail the lines of the future.

Axor slowly got up and, taking the Sceptre of Humility in his hands, the maximum symbol of power, struck the Bell of Light three times. Instants later, as the sound echoed through the chamber, sparking waves of energy in the inner worlds of those gathered there, their meditation manifested itself in a mental image of Ixnor and the Earth ship. Interwoven with this image were various moving spheres representing various Ixnors and various ships in alternative futures, all displayed simultaneously. One of the spheres was a theatre of nuclear explosions and ended in devastation, its inhabitants obliterated; in another sphere, the Crystal Star was targeted and blown to pieces as the Earthmen carried out their final ultimatum; in another, the Earthmen themselves disappeared completely from Ixnor's orbit, disintegrated by the breath of the vibratory power; in yet another, complicated, lengthy negotiations were taking place...

Then Liriel, the Watcher, took the floor. Her soft, measured voice seemed to fill the chamber, resolute, full of power and vehemence yet as peaceful as the planet's mountains.

"Brothers, what we see must now be weighed with our knowledge of the Earthmen's on-going deliberations. We must sound them out, investigate their inner desires and the direction of their free will. This must be done at once. In light of the ethical primitivism we have observed, the situation calls for exceptional measures. I propose scrutiny of the Earthmen."

A short while later (by Earth standards), the navigator was sitting in his detention cell. He felt helpless to alter the course of events. Images of disaster filled his thoughts and, deep down, he cursed himself for having been unable to find the necessary mettle to refuse to help transport this horde of savages through Space. Might he unwittingly become co-responsible for actions on their part that were far worse than those they had already carried out? Then, suddenly, he was aware of a presence. A familiar invigorating presence, a mental breath of fresh air.

Although he couldn't see her, there was no doubt it was Gael. She was there, confirming that she could project her mind across distances, which didn't surprise him in the least. And how good it was to have her near him. Dearest Gael! Then the Interplanetary Welcoming Co-ordinator moved beyond this initial, almost purely affectionate, instant and began to speak with her mind.

"...Dear Henry, you are aware that your Earth brothers are acting in a way which might constitute a threat to us. We have therefore decided to submit all those that have come to Ixnor to scrutiny."

"...What will be done?"

Although he was fearful of the answer, he did not believe the Ixnorians' intentions were hostile.

"...Axor will examine the deep psyche of all those on board. They will be unaware of it. Yet, dear brother, if you agree, in your case it will be different. In fact, it will be hard for you not to be aware of *something*, at the very least. Do you agree to open your inner world to Axor? It won't be like it was with us. It might cause you some pain. With you, the scrutiny could be especially deep. We may be able to learn a large part of Earth's history from what is etched in your soul. In the others, the scrutiny will be more personal and superficial - but it will tell us what we need to know..."

Livingstone did not hesitate. The least he could do was to agree, especially since he found nothing wrong with the idea. Perhaps, in some way, his assent would be taken as a sign of goodwill and would help Axor to see both the good and the bad side of the Earthmen: the navigator had not lost his faith in humanity nor forgotten their capacity for reaching new levels of being...

Then Gael withdrew and the scrutiny began.

Axor made inner contact with him, a vital, powerful and intense presence he had never dreamt he would feel. He felt surrounded by the massive consciousness of the Ixnorian as if nothing else existed... And, abruptly, his deepest thoughts and feelings, his mistakes, his triumphs, his ambitions, what he had said and what, somewhere, he had left unsaid, was suddenly exposed, everything highlighted and concentrated in a timeless space, a sphere of expanded and, in a way, ruthless consciousness. Someone was observing him right down to the tiniest fibres of his being, the molecules of the body, the simplest and most insignificant movements of the psyche. His personal history was all there, present and alive, in all its colours.

That moment at the jazz club, when he had convinced his third girlfriend to go to bed with him. Henry the child on his rocking chair, staring up at the sky and imagining what it would be like if he could rock like that on a cloud. Meditating on top of mountains, on the banks of lakes, in small caves or at home. Incense, experiments with alkaloid drugs under medical control. Depression. Intense joy. Intellectual pride. Instants of humility. That day when he could have helped a friend but hadn't, without even realising as he did now, that he had acted out of selfishness and not the excuse he had given himself. A birthday party he had been to, being held close to his mother's chest. The moment when Bradley and Atkinson had invited him to go on this adventure. Livingstone the young man, moving in the *dojo* of his first karate master, feeling his body sing with the gestures and postures it adopted. Livingstone the student, enthusing about Vedantic philosophy. The child who had been secretly rummaging through his father's things. The fall he had taken trying to jump a fence. Harsh words, sarcastic words, kind words, joyful words, determined words, controversial words. Words... The sounds he had made and those he hadn't made, those he should have made and those he shouldn't. His past and present world of internal and external sounds, his world of feelings, thoughts, actions, truths and lies, intentional or otherwise.

He could not feel more naked, more vulnerable, more confronted with himself. Axor was holding up the supreme mirror to him: his soul looked into it and beheld itself, beyond all escape, subterfuge, defence. Then he felt as if there had been a sudden change in perspective. Axor was now observing him differently.

It was as if, beneath his own thoughts and feelings, the thoughts and feelings of untold generations of human beings on Earth began to arise. His feelings and the feelings of Man. His thoughts and the thoughts of Man. His actions and the actions of Man. Light and mud. Great mystics from the East and West and great exponents of the dark side of humanity. Builders of cathedrals and of souls and destroyers of cities and civilisations. Untold love and untold hate. Massacres and salvation. A symbolic child picking a flower to offer a friend and even displaying ignorance of the vegetable kingdom by doing so. A nuclear mushroom and the screams of millions of human beings. Selfishness and self-denial. Symbolic heroes and real heroes. The betrayal of men, of groups, of nations, of the human race itself. Animals hunted by human predators and abandoned after the slaughter. Sprawling cemeteries filled with the remains of the victims of insane wars, rotting and feeding the soil with disease. A statue of a lady, seemingly forgiving the whole of humanity. Indian burial grounds. Megaliths, pyramids and cathedrals. The thoughts and emotions of individuals, floating in an ocean of thoughts and emotions. A face in a painting, inspiration for generations of human beings. Huge munitions factories. Fragile works of art. Vehicles of all kinds, loud, raucous, belching out their pollution. Discoveries. Technological breakthroughs. Books and reading. Drug traffickers' laboratories. Odes to love. Millions of starving children. The Holy Inquisition preying on some of Earth's finest men. Physical and mental torture. Soulless pornography. Gifts. Theft. Religious hymns. Screams of rage and lynch mobs. Economic dictatorships in the guise of political democracy. Symphonies. The cacophonous screams of bombers. Moments of honour and loyalty to ideals. Sportsmen. Pharmaceutical companies dedicated to making a profit from palliative medicines. Retired men with nothing to do. Meditating monks. Religious fanatics. Trees cut down to serve economic powers. Marches by enthusiastic crowds, inspired, on the road to something precious. Marching armies. Marching multitudes, heads down, fleeing wars, epidemics, natural disasters. Ecologists. Wide-scale corruption and prostitution. Groups of artists devoted to beauty. Borders made and unmade. Religious wars. Territorial wars. Wars. Treaties. Humanitarian organisations. And everything, everything suspended on an immeasurable psychic canvas. Everything laid bare with nothing added, nothing taken away. All of History in all its dynamism concentrated in an instant of pure lucidity.

In his deepest self, Livingstone felt... What did he feel? Who was "he"? He was Earth Humanity and Earth Humanity was he. The whole spectrum of human existence was within him, from the vilest sinner to the most sublime of saints. From the child to the old man. From the caveman to the most spiritual of beings. From the idiot to the intellectual genius. However, between his simultaneously expanded and bared consciousness, there was still room for shame. For the instinctive fear felt by a man who beholds the abyss and knows not what will happen if the abyss beholds him. He felt a stunning range of emotions but, finally, when all that remained was his own consciousness and that of Axor, each facing the other, the Earthman felt the smallness of his own errors, the gravity of those of mankind. Even the psychic irradiation of his own planet shamed him. For an instant, it occurred to him how easy it was to look on Earth and all its inhabitants as polluters and pollution. As the scum of space. The ironic, roaming consequence of a certain piece of space refuse that had one day taught them to travel... Their journey an indirect result of fragments of garbage orbiting the planet Earth. They should never have been given the chance to leave their backward planet and pollute other places. He waited, unable to look up, unable to hold his conscience high before Axor. He waited, fearing a judgement that he would be unable to make given the circumstances.

Then he sat down. Axor did not judge. Not in Livingstone's sense of the word. He did not judge Livingstone and he did not judge the human race. He merely watched, made contact and understood. And acted. At that moment it was as if the Ixnorian were smiling inside his heart, a patriarch patting the head of a naughty child. A child being comforted by his mother. And, at peace, he was immersed in gratitude for having been led far beyond himself. Axor's voice echoed from far away: "I am grateful to you too, my son". How long had all that lasted? It was impossible to tell. Livingstone looked at his watch: three minutes had passed...

One by one, Axor scrutinised the other civilians and military personnel on board the ship. With a few exceptions, none of them noticed anything out of the ordinary; those few that did only had vague, indefinable feelings and spoke of them to no-one. The psychic reality was there, though. The arrogance of the Earth commanders, confident in their power. The numerous, tiny, personal worlds filled with small dreams of greatness and honour on their return to Earth. Those that dreamed of getting rich and, in spite of everything, those that dreamt of discovering or experiencing something truly new, something they could share. Those that had come but feared catching some mysterious disease through contact with the Ixnorians. Those whose irradiation was psychically infectious given the content of their mental emissions. Those that thought they knew it all, blindly trusting their technology, and those that felt worried and ignorant. Many small lives and thoughts. The Earthmen were shut off inside themselves, unable to look at the Cosmos through the eyes of the Cosmos. Instead, they looked on it with their own tiny, fearful, ambitious, paranoid eyes, eyes that were half blind and focused on their personal desires and aversions.

They lacked the dignity of travellers of the Cosmos. Axor ascertained what he needed to, and that included Hamilton Burns "preventive" war plans and the computer programming and simulation of different attacks on Ixnor. Some of them, with the true coldness of military strategy, dared to involve scenarios of total destruction.

On the surface of Ixnor, Diana was relaxing in the room she had been given. She looked out of one of the windows. The view was, as always, breathtaking... Her mind was on other matters, though. The anguish she felt tying her stomach in knots seemed to have one source: the giant orbiting ship. No matter how hard she tried, the Earth officer could find no connection between the fear she felt and the Ixnorians. On the contrary, she was experiencing something of a paradox: she felt more threatened by the Earth commanders than by the supreme leaders of Ixnor, far more threatened by her own people than by the "aliens". Then Gael knocked at her door.

"Sister Diana, I sense your confusion and fear. Let me ask you: are you able internally to determine its source?"

"Yes, I think so, Gael. I'm sorry. I don't quite know what to say. Things aren't going too well between your people and ourselves, and you're smiling as if nothing was wrong... And, in spite of everything, I feel good when I'm with you. I can't believe you'd want to hurt me. And, if you did, I'm not sure that would be wrong. I'm starting to regret having come here. And you... You come to me, let me walk freely among you and don't even ask me to give up my weapons."

"Do not worry. Soon you will understand. And as for your guns, your Earth brothers would consider it treason if you abandoned them, wouldn't they?"

"They would. But if you want me to hand them over to you, I think I can. I don't think they can accuse me of collaborating when I'm alone, with just one other man on the planet."

"I wasn't going to ask you to. But I do have something to ask you. Our leader, Axor, has been carefully observing the inner life of all the Earthmen. Your turn will come shortly. If you wish, we would like your consciousness to accompany the scrutiny. We think that, partly at least, it is viable. Do you agree?"

"But in that case... You know what my commander's plans are?"

Diana's conscience wasn't entirely clear and she was sure that, if she were an Ixnorian and had access to Hamilton Burns' plans, she would at least be worried. Maybe, if she could, she would be preparing for some sort of military intervention.

Gael smiled. Yet no hidden meaning lay behind it. Her tone of voice expressed determination and kindness. A combination that was almost unknown to Diana.

"We know, sister. But this is not the time to talk about it. Do you agree to voluntarily undergo scrutiny?"

Diana trembled. She still hadn't met Axor but, looking at and sensing something in Gael, she could guess what an even partial psychic contact with the planet's supreme leader would be like. Besides, they would clearly find out she had been given orders, to a certain extent, to spy on them. They would also find out that she wasn't making a very good job of it and felt divided. And they must know all this already since they had scrutinised the whole ship. Swallowing dryly, she made her decision. The events that were unfolding were so important, so momentous and her small person was worth nothing.

"I agree. But please: do not judge me harshly... I do the best I can."

The calming smile of the Welcoming Co-ordinator was followed by contact with Axor, whom some Ixnorians called The Watcher.

When it was all over, Diana wept convulsively. She felt crushed within, her ideas a tangled mess. But, when all was said and done, having seen her own potential, her own limitations float before her against a backdrop of such greatness and such misery, a backdrop of life on Earth, having become aware of Axor's incredible tolerance... She began to feel more of a humble apprentice of things Ixnorian than a woman from Earth.

Chapter 16

Divergence and Conflict

Dawn was breaking on Ixnor as the Earthmen landed in the area they had detected and selected from space. The cargo ship took off a short while later leaving behind, amidst the noise and dust, two powerful bulldozers, two drilling machines, four small trucks and diverse mining equipment. Eighty men also remained on the surface, fifty of which were soldiers armed with some of the most powerful portable weapons on Earth. Three fighter ships remained in orbit.

The Earthmen immediately went into action; Fred Bingham, however, the officer in charge of supervising the work, was still receiving the first data on the chemical make-up of the soil and sub-soil when the small Ixnorian ship appeared. Its appearance was not particularly surprising, as it had already been picked up on their monitors. In fact, most of the Earthmen reacted with indifference as it flew over them at low altitude and hung in the air at a height of fifty metres or so. Then a clear, firm voice was heard, one that - surprisingly - seemed neither aggressive nor angry,

"Brothers, you are here without authorisation. We know it is your intention to profane this place by removing various mineral elements and altering the quality of its energy. We ask you to withdraw immediately and return to your own planet."

The officer was clear on the orders he had been given. His voiced sounded tinny and resolute through the powerful megaphone.

"We refuse to withdraw. We believe we have been unjustly treated and as such will only return after we have obtained the minerals we need. *We* ask *you* to leave immediately."

The reply from the Ixnorians was immediate.

"It is not we that should leave. We ask you again not to go ahead with this act of disrespect for the human and non-human inhabitants of Ixnor."

"Refused."

"In that case we will be forced to oppose your actions."

This was followed by a generalised disturbance in the electronic equipment as the ship approached and hovered in the air, motionless, a few metres above the ground. It had stopped directly in front of the mining machinery so as to thwart any attempt to advance. And, indeed, the machines stopped.

Bingham briefed the Earth ship on what had happened.

"Fire a warning shot."

The laser cannons opened up, kicking up clouds of dust next to the Ixnorian ship. The commander of the Earth forces spoke.

"We will not warn you again. You have five minutes to withdraw and cease interfering with our equipment."

The ship remained motionless. Then the same Ixnorian voice sounded.

"We are entitled to defend land that does not belong to you. Once again we ask you to withdraw. We will not leave this area."

Then everything happened quickly. The Earth ship fired its lasers, hitting the small hovering vehicle. It tilted to one side and span drunkenly towards the mining vehicles, their drivers making a quick getaway. Then it fell, as if some anti-gravitational device had suddenly been switched off. The crash completely wrecked one of the bulldozers and damaged two trucks. When the soldiers advanced on the ship in search of prisoners, however, they found it empty.

Bingham contacted Hamilton Burns. The Commander was visibly angry.

"Commander, these clowns sent a robot ship. And it's just destroyed almost half of our mining equipment. It crashed immediately it was hit. I think they set everything up."

"Very well, return at once. We'll pick you up. Things are going to hot up around here now. They should have left us alone."

A short while later, Burns read out a brief communiqué to the civilians and military personnel on board. His face appeared on all the vidcomm monitors around the ship, his impeccable uniform and resolute manners indicative of a warlord convinced of his cause.

"This is Commander Hamilton Burns speaking. A few moments

ago, a small Ixnorian ship crashed into several of our mining vehicles, totally destroying one of them and severely damaging two others. The ship had no crew on board and was operated by remote control. We believe that they set things up so that this would happen as soon as we opened fire on it, which we did after they had provoked us. All we asked was that they let us extract a few minerals from a planet with incalculable reserves, which they have continually refused to do. As you are aware, this is not the first incident they have caused and we have therefore decided to take certain measures. I intend to issue an ultimatum to the effect that they cease all interference and let our two officers on the planet return to the ship. Should they refuse, we shall attack their nerve centre, the Crystal Star, with nuclear weapons. I ask all of you to remain calm. We have reasons to believe that there is nothing on Ixnor to match our ship and that exercising our rights will prove easy. It is unacceptable to us that, having travelled such immense distances through space, we should be subject to such avarice and impudence, and that from the very outset we have been received as half a dozen unimportant individuals from a nearby town. The respect that they have failed to show us will now be imposed. Thank you and the best of luck to all of you."

Then Hamilton Burns contacted Axor.

"Axor, I have just been informed of recent events and demand an immediate explanation."

"There is nothing to explain. You landed on our planet in order to steal our minerals without permission and without taking into account our request for careful assessment of the situation. One of your men behaved unacceptably beforehand to Gael, and all she did was defend herself without causing any injury. What sort of an explanation were you hoping for?"

"You know full well that you prepared your ship for the eventuality of an attack and that important equipment was destroyed. We were provoked and, when we tried to defend ourselves, that was the result. It's obvious that you didn't send a manned ship because you knew what you were going to do with it."

"That is correct, my brother. We knew it might be attacked. Yet we did not prepare it to bring about destruction. That was simply an avoidable consequence of your aggressiveness. And your aggressiveness forces me to ask you to return to your own planet."

"Not so fast. We'll do that once we've got what we want. For the time being, I demand that the two Earthmen on Ixnorian soil be returned at once. I shall be sending a new mining crew to the same location and if you interfere this time I shall destroy the Crystal Star. Have I made myself clear?"

Axor's expression did not change, his young, serene face standing out against the bright background of the room in which he sat. His voice, though still calm, had taken on a subtly different tone. And that tone expressed firmness. Nothing more than firmness.

"What you are doing goes against all our ethics. Obviously your brothers may return immediately if that is what they want. As for the mining crew, we will not allow such activity and will not allow them to land on Ixnor. I ask you to think carefully about what you are saying."

"I have. I repeat: do not interfere or we shall destroy the Crystal Star."

"My brother, if you attempt to carry out such a threat, we shall be forced to destroy all your equipment. We do not wish to use aggression but, if it proves unavoidable, we will defend ourselves."

"Should I take it that you are threatening to use military action against us?"

"No, my brother, you should not. All I am saying is that any new aggression on your part will result in the total destruction of your equipment."

Hamilton Burns could hardly believe it. The man had to be bluffing: Star 1's scanners continued to show that everything was normal on Ixnor, no large vessels, no weapons. But he decided to give them some time to reflect and to come to their senses.

"I shall pass this on to my advisors. In the meantime, I shall take it as a temporary act of goodwill on your part if you let our soldiers return to the ship."

"So be it. I shall wait to hear from you again. You have ten hours."

"What? Now you're imposing a deadline?"

"Take it as you want. With one, perhaps two exceptions, your presence on Ixnor is no longer desirable."

"And who's the exception?"

"Your navigator, Henry Livingstone. You know that full well. I suggest you give him the option of staying on Ixnor if he wishes."

"Ah, I see. And how would we return without our navigator?"

"Do not try to lie, my brother. There's no point. You know that you have various crew members on board that can translocate the ship back to Earth."

How the hell did they know that? Hamilton Burns was becoming increasingly more angry. The smooth-talking leader threatening him and accusing him of lying was testing his patience. He decided to leave it there, though.

"We will consider what you have said. Out."

Half an hour later, the Commander met with his officers. Diana had returned to the ship and had been asked to attend the briefing. Burns took the floor.

"Very well, you are all aware of what happened and the content of my conversation with Axor. I want to hear your comments."

Jim Dawson spoke first.

"Can we really be certain that their threat is just a bluff? I've only met Axor once, but he doesn't seem the bluffing type. It's possible that he really believes they can carry out their threat. And, if you think about it, it is their planet..."

"Impossible. They have no heavy weaponry, perhaps not even any light weapons. They may even be a race of dreamers. Whatever the case, they have shown that they can destroy our equipment by sacrificing their ships and that they possess sophisticated electronic jamming equipment. So we must not forget that when we begin mining they may attack us. And I intend to avoid it."

Then the direct representative of the president of the United States, William Burns, intervened.

"Why don't we ask them to supply us with the minerals we need and remove them from an area of their choosing? They appear to have reasons we are unaware of for wanting to avoid indiscriminate mining..."

"We have chosen a quiet, unpopulated area, one that is extremely rich. I wouldn't call that indiscriminate. Anyway, Axor was clear on one thing: they want to drive us away. Besides, the way we've been treated warrants our taking a tough stand. We will not return with our tail between our legs!"

"...But does that justify destroying a work of art as stunning as the Crystal Star?"

"Mr. Bates, may I remind you that they have already destroyed equipment belonging to us and that the only reason no-one was killed was because they managed to get away in time. If they want to avoid this, it's easy: they just don't interfere."

"Commander, may I suggest we hear what Diana has to say? She was down there for quite a while, after all, and may be able to add something."

It was John McPherson that had spoken, the youngest of the officers. And Diana, who had almost prayed not to be consulted, swallowed dryly.

"Agreed, Diana?" Burns asked.

She began to speak. What the hell, she'd say what she felt was right for a change.

"I'm sorry, Commander, but I think we're acting like barbarians. They are on their planet and are entitled to decide what is or isn't acceptable to them."

"Is that so?" Fred Bingham asked. "And what gives them the right to mistreat us or attack our ground forces?"

Diana was indignant.

"I believe we opened fire first. I see nothing that demonstrates bad faith on their part."

"There's something very odd here", said the Commander. "Why on earth are you defending them? How were you treated down there? Did they brainwash you or something?"

"They did no such thing. For your information, Commander, I've never been so well treated nor so respected in all my life!"

"I want you to report at once to the on-duty psychiatrist for a thorough check-up. I suspect they've done something to you. Let's see what our other envoy has to say. Homer?"

The attitude of the other officer that had stayed behind on the planet was quite different. He was still interested in his career and thought it best to go with the flow...

"We were reasonably well treated, although we were left somewhat - how shall I put it - to our own devices."

Diana was about to protest, but a gesture from the Commander cut her short.

"...I actually think they were too kind. I fear that for some time they have been planning something, though I don't know what. But it's clear they're telepathic and may even be picking up what we're saying right now. They communicate with each other practically without words."

"I believe we have heard enough", said Burns. "I propose we respect the deadline we've been given to the second to give us time to plan an attack on the Crystal Star. I don't believe it will be necessary to carry it out, especially if they are reading my thoughts," he added, smiling maliciously. "We shall contact Axor and, if he has not changed his position by then, we attack."

As he contacted Axor again a few moments later, Burns felt completely in his element. He was reminded of the Arab-American war...

"Very well, Axor, that's the way things stand. What do you intend to do?"

"Absolutely nothing except wait. Everything I said still stands. Unfortunately, we will be forced to destroy your equipment if you opt to attack. I once again insist that you return to Earth. You have done enough to become undesirable."

"If that's your final word, we will be forced to change your minds through the use of force. We demand authorisation to set down a mining crew and the promise that you will not interfere."

"I refuse. I am afraid that we will shortly be forced to take definitive measures concerning you."

Later, when the communication had ended, Burns gave orders for two nuclear missiles to be prepared, their target the Crystal Star. Their trajectories were calculated and fighter planes were readied to prevent the missiles from being shot down. The countdown began.

One thing still had to be cleared up, though: why were they so taken with the navigator? What did he have to do with recent events? And what had they done to Diana?

"Dawson, bring Livingstone to me. I want to talk to him. Fill him in on what's happened. I don't want to waste time discussing useless things with him. As for Diana, I want a complete medical report within the hour."

When he arrived, Livingstone was still confused, stunned. Why on earth was Burns unable to see what he was doing? He remained confused as various electrodes were attached to his body and his head, a microphone placed near his mouth. In a few moments he would be ready to answer - according to the technicians. His galvanic response, his electroencephalographic patterns, the spread of his brain activity and vocal parameters were all being monitored. Any attempt at lying or concealing the truth would trigger a change in his central nervous system and sympathetic and parasympathetic systems, originating the need to conserve or expend energy when certain questions were asked (he would feel stressed if there was a difference between what he was saying and the truth, for example, or calm if he was not lying). General fluctuations, both voluntary and involuntary, in muscular tension coupled with his electroencephalographic patterns may also be accompanied by vocal tremors and subtle changes in his voice timbre, all this in relation to the content of his replies. Hamilton Burns felt confident that it he tried to lie, they would know. Cases of the people that had been able to fool the technical apparatus they were using were almost non-existent.

For the navigator, the whole set-up was both nightmarish and farcical. If they knew him at all well, they would know he never lied. He looked on lying as something base, the brutal opposite of one of the things that the human race needed most: truth. So, when he began to speak, he did so with determination and the secret satisfaction of knowing that, if he told the commander what he thought of him, he would know that was really what he thought...

"Commander Burns, what you are doing is monstrous and unworthy of us. I ask you to reconsider."

The commander cut him off.

"We are in a state of war and you were not called here to argue. I want to know why they want you down there."

"I've no idea. Unless it's because they find me different from you. They know that I support none of this. They also know I am being held prisoner. Maybe they think that's a mistake."

"Just that? They're being kind, they feel sorry for you?" Burns couldn't help smiling, a smile that poked fun.

"Believe what you want. If you really want to know, Commander, I am more than willing to return you to Earth before you do any more damage. As for what you think of me or what happens to me afterwards, I really couldn't care."

"We'll deal with that later. Your answer is totally unacceptable to me. You didn't pass on any information you shouldn't have, by any chance?"

"What information? You know very well I've never had access to any of your military secrets."

Burns looked at his technicians, who were closely following the electromyographic, electroencephalographic and electroacoustic read-outs of Livingstone's muscular and cerebral activity. It seemed likely that was he was telling the truth. One of the technicians, a satisfied look on his face, even gave Burns a thumbs up, which angered the Commander.

"So you stick by what you're saying? You have no idea?"

"I only know what I've told you. Is telling the truth now a crime here too?"

"I suggest you watch what you say and think long and hard. I shall investigate the matter, and you may even be charged with treason. You appear to be siding with those smooth-talking curs. Until then, you will remain under arrest. And by the way, we don't need your services to return home. We have other possibilities."

"I thought you might. You wouldn't treat me like this if you needed me."

"Don't bet on it... Dawson, please escort our ex-navigator back to his cell."

Hamilton Burns signalled Randolph Skinner, the technician in charge of monitoring the interrogation, to approach him.

"Well, Randolph?"

"The man did okay, Commander. He was clearly irritated but there was no discrepancy between his brain patterns and what he was saying. I've rarely seen such coherence between hemispheres of the brain, general activity of the nervous system and expression. That's some guy, I can tell you."

Burns didn't like the man's idiotic smile, but had to accept the evidence as it was presented. Skinner was an expert, after all.

"Very well. Thank you. You may leave."

Sitting in a corner of the bridge, Diana tried to get a grip on herself. She felt like smashing everything in sight, but she couldn't. Only a few tears, which ran silently down her face, gave any indication that she was not all right. She was sad she wasn't on Ixnor, in the City of Water, and couldn't tell the Ixnorians that she had nothing to do with what was happening. Deep down, however, something told her they knew.

For Livingstone, the next hour passed agonisingly slowly. He was aware of the mental powers of the Ixnorians but wasn't sure they could prevent the attack. Besides, he knew them well enough to know that if they believed deep inside that they were right, they would never give in to threats. Then, once again, he felt Gael's unmistakable presence. He knew that his cell was being monitored, but, luckily, they communicated with their minds, and it was far beyond the powers of the Earthmen to detect what they were saying.

"... I know you are suffering but you need not worry. The attack will not take place. I assure you. Now I must carry on dealing personally with the matter. We shall speak again in a few hours. Trust me, please."

In spite of everything, the hours that followed were torturous. The approach of the deadline set by Axor and adopted by Burns now seemed to be beaten out with a hammer. He regretted coming and helping the Earthmen come to Ixnor, he blamed himself and blamed himself again for his lack of judgement. Then, glancing at his watch every now and then, he waited as time slowly, slowly ran out. When the hour finally came, he merely asked what he thought of as God, to kill him if needs be, but not to let anything happen to the Ixnorians. Then everything happened at once.

On the bridge, Burns gave out his orders.

"Dawson, arm and prepare the missiles. I want the trajectories double-checked and a final read-out on activity on Ixnor."

A few seconds passed.

"Confirmed. And there's no detectable change in activity on Ixnor."

Diana could restrain herself no longer.

"Commander, what you are about to do is atrocious. I'll have no part in this pointless slaughter! As of now I resign, whether you like it or not." Then, looking around her, she cried: "I call on all of you here to disobey this monster before it's too late!"

Burns reacted quickly and angrily.

"Diana, you're under arrest! Guards, take her away. You'll be sentenced later."

Then, as the insubordinate was forcibly removed from the bridge, the Commander gave the order for the missiles to be launched, the deadline seconds away. Two men approached the commands as his voice cut through the tomb-like silence that had descended on the ship: "10, 9, 8, 7..."

He never got to zero. Moments before, a powerful whistling

sound was heard which resounded throughout the ship, seeming to penetrate the very bones of the Earthmen. Sitting in his cell, Livingstone became aware that something very subtle but extremely powerful had been unleashed. He felt calm, though, and profoundly indifferent to the fact that he may or may not be dead within a few seconds. Then there was a bright flash. And everyone lost consciousness...

Chapter 17

The Return

Axor and the Council had felt the need to question the logic of Space and to contemplate the silent Mind that guided the destiny of the Universe. How had these human beings, most of them so primitive, been allowed to reach their planet? What was the sense in their discovering the secret of space translocation?

The answer was clear, firm: mankind on Earth was at a transitional stage, one that would result in their opening up to the Cosmos, both internally and externally. Many humans on Earth were starting to sense the ocean of possibilities inside themselves and that they must "journey into their inner worlds" before they could journey through space. Many were beginning to find, within themselves, the roots of true solidarity and were developing a sensitivity to "the language of things and beings" - to the energetic vibration on a far wider spectrum than they or others had experienced before. And there was a man on board that enormous Earth ship who, centuries before and in a different body, had been on Ixnor. Livingstone had known Gael and other Ixnorians long before the onset of the unfortunate events that were now taking place. And it made sense that such apparently fortuitous circumstances, albeit guided by the logic of Space, had brought him to Ixnor - a planet with which he shared a great affinity. Everything seemed to indicate that, in a more or less remote future, he would return to Earth. When this happened, he would assume a special role since that would be the moment when most Earthmen (and not just a few) would start to become aware of the profound nature that linked them to the conscious Cosmos. Livingstone, the traveller, would help mankind to "return to the Universe". And then there was Diana, the young girl from Earth that had yet to discover her real self but could if she wished. She could also choose between returning to her physical planet or life on Ixnor... Besides, quite unexpectedly, many of the Earthmen that now seemed so aggressive, so out of sync with the Ethics of the Cosmos, would take with them a psychic reminder of what they had seen and experienced. A secret psychic mark, and one day that mark would make itself heard and remind them of other ways of being. Having known another way of vibrating with life, they would never again lose the gift of recognising it...

Livingstone gently regained consciousness. He felt slightly bewildered. His eyes were still closed as he remembered the final seconds of consciousness. The whistling, the flash and the sensation that, whatever was happening, it was better than allowing an absurd nuclear attack against Ixnor to go ahead. Then, propping himself up on one elbow, he looked around. The planet's sun had begun to rise above the horizon, casting its light on an incredible scene: he was on the surface of Ixnor and, on this same surface, scattered over a wide, flat area covered in vegetation, thousands of Earthmen began to move vaguely about. Here and there groans, cries of despair could be heard. The navigator then noticed something else: there were only humans there, dressed in the clothes they were wearing before the end of the countdown for the attack on Ixnor. There were no weapons. No vehicles. No insignia. No machines of any sort. And, everywhere, thousands of stunned people looked around and looked to the skies in search of an explanation.

The navigator smiled, satisfied. It was obvious that the Ixnorians had taken care of the threat, and probably without death or injury, without pain and without suffering. If that was how they waged war, good on them!

A few hundred metres away, however, he saw a larger concentration of people. Some were shouting. He jumped to his feet and approached them. In the centre of the group was Hamilton Burns, looking most unsure of himself. The same went for his officers, who seemed to have very little idea what to do next. Some other officers and soldiers were about to discover something to do, though. That, at least, was what the clenched jaws and closed fists seemed to indicate. And various illustrative phrases could be heard...

"You bastard! We're done because of you!"

"This was our power, was it? Son of a bitch!"

"What now? You said they were no match for us. Any idea what they're going to do to us, too?"

"And just how do I get home, dear Commander?"

"These sorcerers can wipe us out when they want; lend me your laser, Commander?"

Livingstone moved closer. Fearing a lynching, he spoke up,

"Enough! Stop doing things you might regret later. Can we just stop and think for a while? Has anyone been hurt or killed? All I see are doubts and headaches! Maybe that should cheer you up a bit, don't you think?"

The mob stared at him, surprised, not knowing what to say. Burns was not lost for words, though. His voice was clear and cutting.

"Dawson, Bingham, grab that man. He's got some explaining to do about his Ixnorian buddies. Harmless, weren't they?"

Seeing a few unarmed soldiers approach him as a tomb-like silence descended for several metres around him, faces staring at each other as if trying to decide what to do, the navigator braced himself. Would he now have to fight for his life? These people were seriously upset...

"Grab me? What for? There's thousands of us here, none of us knows what's going to happen next; do you think you'll solve anything by looking for scapegoats?"

Burns sought to retain the initiative. It was clearly best to divert attention away from himself and direct the anger and anguish of the mob at another target.

"I doubt they'll be wanting to treat us nicely. But you've got some explaining to do. You could have warned us and you didn't. I bet you knew what they were capable of, what they were up to. That makes you a traitor. Get him, you cowards! The man has to be brought to justice."

Livingstone prepared to fight for his life when he remembered Gael and the other Ixnorians. They must know what was going on. If they didn't intervene, they must have their reasons. Besides, he'd had enough already. What was the sense in answering violence with violence? He dropped his guard. He was about to say something when the first soldier caught him with a vicious hook to the stomach. He doubled up, protecting himself with his hands as another soldier grabbed him from behind. It occurred to him that these could be the last few seconds of his life as he felt the group close in around him. Then he heard a powerful, unmistakable voice ring out, almost metallic in tone.

"Enough! Leave him be!"

A scant thirty metres away, in the middle of the agitated Earthmen, the Planetary Council of Ixnor had appeared out of thin air. It was Axor that had spoken and confronted with his powerful voice, which seemed to have blown like a fearful wind through their own consciousness... no-one dared move. Livingstone managed a slight smile as he looked at these men and women, simply dressed in white tunics, their hands held before them, calm but determined.

Axor moved forward and stopped a short distance from Hamilton Burns. Then suddenly, one of the Earth soldiers ran at the Ixnorian, his fists raised.

"You're the guy that's gonna waste us, are you? Well, you go first!"

A few metres behind, Zultar, the Guardian, let out a short, powerful sound as he extended his right arm, his hand open, towards the soldier and lifted his left hand towards the sky, his elbow bent at an angle. Livingstone felt the breath of The Power as he watched, feeling no need to intervene, the events unfolded. It was obvious that the Ixnorians had reached a point where they would no longer tolerate such behaviour.

The soldier seemed to run into an invisible wall. He fell backwards, without touching Axor, and lay still. His body was smoking. A companion bent over him and felt the pulse in his neck. He was dead. Then Zultar's voice rang out again, in a tone that the navigator could only describe as tempestuous. It was evident that all of the thousands of Earthmen gathered there were able to hear him, his voice seeming to echo inside and outside their skulls, spreading throughout the area like a powerful vibrating wave.

"I AM ZULTAR, THE GUARDIAN. WE SHALL NOT CONSENT TO ANY MORE AGGRESSION. NO MORE DISTORTION AND VIOLENCE!"

Then Axor, who had remained motionless during the attack, spoke up again. His eyes flashed as he spoke, his voice prolonging and developing the irresistible effect of Zultar's words. It was impossible not to listen to him, feel him, pay attention to him. There was no way, nowhere to run from the sound of a thought that judged without condemning - but that judged and deliberated according to an inhuman logic. The Earthmen suddenly felt like tiny, tiny children.

"You came to Ixnor with hidden intentions. You thought of us with the blindness of an egocentric and selfish thought. Your actions were primitive and sought to rob and profane instead of respecting our freewill and our science. Even the knowledge that brought you to Ixnor was the result of a circumstance exempt of merit.

"Your civilisation has spawned noble men but it has also spawned criminals, and has not yet found a balance which will allow it to ascend to the Cosmos with true dignity. You are still, in part, parasites of your own planet. On a physical level, you produce refuse that breaks the cycle of natural renovation. On a psychic level, you produce mental and emotional refuse, energy that infects and pollutes the spiritual environment. You bring with you the same tendencies as your animal ancestors - only masked and expressed intellectually. You have responded to respect and simplicity with complex machinations that are the mark of your pre-cosmic civilisation. In your relationships you still look on each other as mere bodies, mere psychic and biological agglomerations. Your selfishness makes the power you possess dangerous. Your weapons of destruction are indicative of a selfishness and an aggressiveness that are incompatible with the gift of traversing Time and Space. You have committed crimes against harmony.

"In light of all this, your biomagnetic irradiation, the psychic content of your mental and emotional worlds, the lack of refinement of your senses and your mental apparatus, your unawareness, we have been forced, against our will, to defend ourselves. This makes the presence amongst us of most of those that came on the ship - which we have to reduce to a state of potential - intolerable. With two exceptions - if they agree - you will immediately be sent back to the planet Earth."

Then his expression changed, became softer, as his voice ever so slightly changed tone. There was no need to be more determined than he had to.

"One day, brothers, we will welcome you with the same joy and the same openness. Then we will be able to share that which we have been unable to share. One day you will bring to us the fire of knowledge that will have been awakened in you and our reunion will be mutually enriching. What I do is not incompatible with love. What is happening is simply a postponement of the communion. Our blessing will go with you despite the fact that harsh actions have proved necessary. We salute in you the promise of the consciousness of children of the Cosmos."

"How can that be?" asked Burns, distressed. "How can we return? What's become of our ship? Will it be returned to us?"

"Your ship and all your technical equipment have been reduced to a formless state of energy. This would not have happened if you had not turned your ships' weapons on us and had not attempted to use your equipment to profane the surface of Ixnor. You will be returned, as a group, to your planet."

Burns still tried to react, still tried ridiculously to take control of the situation.

"...And if we refuse to go?"

"You have no choice. You have no say in the matter. We shall not allow any further acts of aggression and shall look on any attempt to resist as such. We ask you to co-operate so that we may send you back in safety."

"What do we do with the dead soldier? We have no means of transporting him."

"If you wish his body to be sent back to Earth, we can do that too."

"Very well. I think it would be best to bury him on our own planet."

"So be it then. He will go with you. Anyway, I believe I can tell you that, at this moment in time, he feels better. One of our Ixnorian elders is looking after him."

"What?!"

"I know you are not aware of the continuity of life. You don't even realise that your body is temporary and will be replaced by another later, when you have learnt something else. But that's the way it is."

The conversation didn't last much longer. There wasn't much to say, given that Hamilton Burns didn't comprehend and didn't want deeper communication with the Ixnorians. Then Gael stepped forward between the motionless Earthmen - still unable to digest recent events - and reached out to Livingstone, who took her hand with a smile. Then she stepped a few more paces silently forward, Livingstone by her side, and reached out to Diana. The young officer sighed, caught between anguish and intense joy, and took her hand. She too had made her choice. Gael moved away with them, accompanied by most of the Planetary Council.

Axor spoke again.

"We will place a series of resonators around this field. Then all of you that are to return to your planet will be put to sleep. You will be projected to a pre-designated point on your planet. Anyone that attempts to escape from the area bounded by the resonators will meet with instant death."

Hamilton Burns was about to speak; Axor cut him off.

"You have said all you have to say. We do not believe you are yet in a position to produce anything really new. Perhaps in some years..."

There was no anger in his voice. There was no weakness or hesitation, either. Burns felt it would be best not to push his luck. If they really were simply going to be sent back, unharmed, to their planet, perhaps that was reasonable. He had lost the battle and there was nothing else he could do, for the time being at least...

Then various Ixnorian vessels landed on the edge of the grassy field. Several groups of men and women descended from them and quickly placed various small apparatus in position. Then, as Axor and Liriel remained in the centre of the area, the devices began to emit a series of powerful vibrations. At a distance, Livingstone and Diana felt the ground beneath their feet enter into resonance as, one by one, the Earthmen in the field began to lay down.

Travor, the elder, let the telepathic connection go on for a while longer. The soldier Frazer wasn't sure of what would happen next and felt incapable of returning to Earth by his own means.

"...You just need to stay here with your companions. We'll take care of the rest. Just let yourself go and focus on the fact that you're going with them."

"...Thank you. And I'm sorry. I didn't know it was like this..."

"...May your apprenticeship remain with you. Go in peace."

Hamilton Burns felt an incredible drowsiness come over him. He tried vainly to resist, cursing inside his tiny, paranoid mind. When he awoke, he was surrounded by thousands of sleepy humans returned from afar in a place that was easily identifiable. Looking around, he recognised the Pentagon. And several guards pointing their guns in all directions, amazed...

On another level, Frazer also recognised where he was. However, looking around, he saw his father appear. He hadn't seen him since he had been killed in an accident 17 years earlier. He was accompanied by Phillip, a faithful friend that had been killed during the Arab-American war.

"Good to see you again, Frazer. But where did you die this time? We hadn't heard anything about you until a while ago..."

Moments later, above the planet Earth, the small Ixnorian ship that had remained in orbit moved off and translocated back to Ixnor. It left behind no trace of its presence. No ship was detected. The sudden and total disappearance of all the plans and documents on spatial translocation as well as all experimental vehicles and research structures connected with it remained unexplained. As did the strange inability on the part of the technicians to remember exactly what they had been studying in this field. Commander Burns learnt, a few weeks later, that they would not be able to return to Ixnor. Not even to leave the solar system...

Chapter 18

Spiritual Homeland

For the very first time in his life, Henry Livingstone was seriously confronted with the possibility of spending the rest of his life on another planet, in another place in the universe. Before, this had been nothing more than the vaguest of possibilities in his mind's horizon, now it had become a fact. His responsibility towards the Earthmen he had translocated across Space had come to an end and, with it, he was experiencing a hitherto unfound freedom. There was still some fear, on a personal level, in view of the unknown. There was still the impact of a planet where the vibration was far more powerful than on Earth. But deep inside, as each instant passed, his joy continued to grow. In his body, he still felt like a stranger; in his mind, he felt as if he had returned home to his native planet. There were various reasons for this and one of them had to do with the fact that the Ixnorians felt like citizens of the universe and enjoyed sharing their city, whilst most Earthmen still clung to their delimited territories, whether these were physical or psychological.

The ex-navigator was back in the City of Water again, dressed in a gold tunic, in the same room that had been given him when he had arrived - the room where he had really come to know Gael. Now, as he serenely awaited the Welcoming Co-ordinator, the woman that was to become his wife, he recalled not only that special moment but also the succession of events that had turned him into a citizen of Ixnor.

At the end, he had made telepathic contact with Axor and come to understand much of what had passed. The Planetary Leader had explained as best he could the nature of "the Mind of Space" and how this strange entity that seemed to preside over the Spatial-Temporal unfolding of the infinite lines of potential events, had allowed the Earthmen to journey to Ixnor and, beforehand, had permitted them to successfully attempt translocation. He had explained the way in which even an ant should be taken into account in the infinite scheme of macrocosmic events. And then he had revealed to him the nature of the "weapon" - as the Earth military thought of it - used to ensure that nothing would be done to harm their planet.

On an energy level that was far too subtle to be detected by Star 1's instruments, the Planetary Council had constructed a "form abstracting field of light". This mental creation, patterned according to all the objects and devices that would have to be destroyed if necessary, had been set up in such a way that it would be triggered by the Earthmen's own destructive intent should they try to launch their attack on Ixnor. So, as the countdown to the attack on the Crystal Star approached zero and the Commander's finger moved ever closer to the missile launch panel, the energy field, activated by Hamilton Burns' own brain waves, kicked into action - dematerialising the whole of the ship and its technical equipment. At the same time, another "field of light" had been prepared to instantly put the Earthmen to sleep and beam them down to a point on the surface of Ixnor that had been chosen for the nature of its vibration. It would then be possible to send the Earthmen back to their home planet. All this, which had involved so much time and energy, was destined to take place only in the event that the free will of the Earthmen led them to choose the path of violence. Unfortunately, this was exactly what had happened.

Afterwards, an Ixnorian ship had journeyed to Earth to make sure that the secret of translocation would only be rediscovered when the Earthmen found it as a natural consequence of being in harmony with themselves, with the planet and with cosmic Space.

How Livingstone's life on Ixnor was going to be was something he still did not know. But neither he nor the Ixnorians were in any hurry. For now, the most important thing was to learn. To learn a lot, to feel a lot, to live among them. Later, as he began to settle down, he would be able to choose a line of work with which he felt the greatest affinity. In the meantime, there was something that would help make him a part of the planet. Livingstone was to be married - and this time a cliché in many Earth novels was in fact true: he really was going to marry the woman of his dreams...

When Gael arrived, bringing Livingstone out of his daydreaming, he felt a wave of contagious happiness take hold of him. He had no trouble returning it as he felt the warm embrace of the woman he loved. The Interplanetary Welcoming Co-ordinator was wearing a gold tunic, similar to his own, and she seemed even prettier on that morning than before. Was he being objective or sentimental? Was it true, as a wise man from Earth had once said, that only love could make people really objective?

A short while later, in the middle of the Norya Plateau - the place they had both chosen for the ceremony - they sat facing each other in meditation, joined once more in the most intimate of their energies, their personal and impersonal histories, the cores of their biophysical and spiritual activity. In a triangle around them a few metres away, Axor, Liriel and Aila, the Ethics Officiant, peacefully accompanied the moment. They were at once friends, best men and bridesmaids, guests, and something more than this. They were also mentors and companions. The small group was made complete by the timid presence of Diana, who felt like laughing, crying and hugging them all at the same time, and a few Ixnorians who, in a sense, were relatives and friends of Gael and friends of both. The music of nature, composed of the soft wind, the chirp of birds and a subtle vibration that the bride and groom heard from within, set the right tone as Gael and Livingstone emerged from their concentration in a state of heightened awareness.

The three mentors approached and then, smiling, asked them:

"Do you wish to now make this moment whole and cause this bond of freedom to flow?"

The answer was joyous and easy.

"We now make this bond of freedom whole. Before the multiple spheres of the soul on Ixnor, before nature, before the Cosmos."

"I consecrate myself to you, Gael."

"I consecrate myself to you, Livingstone."

"We consecrate ourselves to humanity, to Life and to the Cosmos. May our energy follow the paths of Righteousness, Service and Happiness."

Then, in silence, the three mentors reached out their hands towards the couple, their fingers spread out in a fan shape, and offered them the blessing of their energy as they uttered the simple phrase:

"So be it."

The wedding had taken place. All that remained was life and living, symbolised in the dance-like movements of all those present, twisting in a spiral that spread out around Gael and Livingstone.

A few metres away, Twick, one of nature's small beings, peeked out from behind some bushes. He had no means of describing or analysing what was going on but, whatever it was, he felt like joining in the dancing with the other beings there. His harmony had returned - and it grew as he saw them calmly move off in a silent ship.

Diana was still bewildered at the succession of events. Slowly, however, it all began to sink in. She too had journeyed under the burden of psychic disharmony and paranoia that still partially reigned on Earth. And yet, by letting her inner self speak and open up to the attempt to feel the Ixnorians as they had presented themselves, knowing them instead of fearing them or withdrawing from them, she felt far more cherished and understood than she had ever felt throughout the irregular course of her life. Staying here seemed the only viable alternative after the attitude she had adopted during the final stage of the relations between her Earth companions and the Ixnorians; nevertheless, it was also probably a much better choice than returning to Earth, even if it were a triumphant return, filled with honour and acclaim.

And there had been the wedding, which had reconciled her fully with the idea of the institution of matrimony - provided it didn't conform to several of the Earth examples - and had filled her with an even greater gratitude for being there. And then there was Tumir. She felt extremely attracted to the man that had invited her to a certain concert and who, as she had later found out, was an artist in a sense she had never known on Earth. His work consisted in studying the fine energy currents that existed in selected areas of the planet, rich in fertile land, and, when appropriate, concentrating them and directing them in such a way as to produce particularly beautiful plants. This sometimes involved scientific and artistic skills, rearranging natural stones, using them as accumulators and diffusers of energy, and, in collaboration with the subtle beings known as the "Builders of Vegetable Forms", mentally creating morphogenetic patterns which gave vegetables particularly harmonious appearances. Diana, who had always been a bit of a rebel, always quick to react aggressively, now felt attracted by the "art of natural forms". And she had someone to teach her. Apart from the fact that Tumir, with the typical naturalness of the Ixnorians, had told her: "I should like to get to know you better, my sister. I feel that, between us, the paths of love can join in harmony".

For the first time she could remember, despite the maelstrom of events in which she had been caught up, she felt at peace, truly at peace with herself, no more, no less. And it was quite simply, indescribably, good...

The End.

FOR MORE INFORMATION ABOUT BOOKS PUBLISHED, VITOR CAN BE CONTACTED THROUGH HIS WEB SITE

http://vitorrodriguesen.weebly.com/

http://www.innervisionpress.com

Lightning Source UK Ltd.
Milton Keynes UK
UKOW01f0327150816

280640UK00001BA/109/P